THE
MIDNIGHT
LIBRARY

—

Shut your Mouth

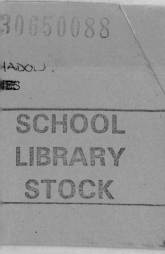

THE MIDNIGHT LIBRARY

Shut your Mouth

Nick Shadow

Hodder
Children's
Books

A division of Hodder Headline Limited

Special thanks to Sally Jones
and Allan Frewin Jones

Text copyright © 2006 Working Partners Limited
Illustration copyright © 2006 David McDougall
Created by Working Partners Limited, London W6 0QT

First published in Great Britain in 2006
by Hodder Children's Books

1

A Catalogue record for this book is available from
the British Library

ISBN 0 340 89410 5

Typeset in Weiss Antiqua by Avon DataSet Ltd,
Bidford-on-Avon, Warwickshire

Printed and bound in Great Britain by
Clays Ltd, St Ives plc

The paper and board used in this paperback by
Hodder Children's Books are natural recyclable products
made from wood grown in sustainable forests. The manufacturing
processes conform to the environmental regulations
of the country of origin.

Hodder Children's Books
a division of Hodder Headline Limited
338 Euston Road
London NW1 3BH

Welcome, reader.

My name is Nick Shadow,
curator of that secret
institution:

The Midnight Library

Where is the Midnight Library, you ask?
Why have you never heard of it?
For the sake of your own safety, these questions are better left
unanswered. However … so long as you promise not to reveal
where you heard the following (no matter who or *what*
demands it of you), I will reveal what I
keep here in the ancient vaults.
After many years of searching,
I have gathered the most terrifying
collection of stories known to
man. They will chill you to
your very core, and make
flesh creep on your young,
brittle bones. Perhaps you should
summon up the courage and turn the
page. After all, what's the worst that
could happen … ?

M L

The Midnight Library: Volume VI

Stories by Sally Jones and Allan Frewin Jones

CONTENTS

SHUT YOUR MOUTH

'Hey, you! What are you doing?'

Louise nearly leaped out of her skin. Niki, Laura and Sarah had crept up behind her as she sat waiting for them in the park. She'd been talking to a little kid who was giving her toy rabbit a ride on the swings and Niki had bellowed right into her ear. Niki, Laura and Sarah doubled over, laughing and pointing.

'Very funny – not,' Louise muttered, trying to

keep her cool. From where she was sitting, it seemed as though Niki towered over her, red hair fizzing out from her head like a fiery halo. Louise knew that Niki could be a real laugh, but it was normally only if you went along with what *she* wanted to do.

'Your face!' Laura was saying, spitting out the words between giggles. 'You went like . . . *oooh* . . . *wuh* . . .' And she opened her mouth in a big 'O', flashing the braces on her teeth.

'Oi, you – off the swing!' Niki said. Louise watched as she marched up to the little girl. 'And take your stupid fluffy rabbit with you!' she finished, batting the little girl's toy on to the ground.

Louise hated it when Niki got like this. 'Just leave it, Niki—' she began, but Laura interrupted her.

'Can't you see the notice?' Laura chimed in. ' "No animals allowed"!'

'But . . . it's not a real animal,' the little girl murmured. Louise could see that the girl was intimidated by the others. Her face had drained of

2

colour, and she kept staring up quickly, and then returning her gaze to the floor.

'Still counts as an animal if it's got four legs and a tail, I'm afraid,' Sarah said, pretending to look very serious.

'Hey, girls, let's leave her alone. She's not doing any harm,' Louise said, trying to distract Niki and the others.

'Just get off the swing, kid, and disappear,' Niki said, blanking Louise completely.

At that moment, Louise saw a woman walking over towards the swings at a brisk pace. *Thank goodness – this must be her mum*, Louise thought. *She'll put Niki in her place*. As the woman approached, Niki leaned down close to the little girl.

'Mind you don't go blabbing to your mum!' she hissed in her ear, and the girl pulled away as though she'd been stung, and ran off.

'Looks like she's just seen the wicked witch!' Sarah giggled.

'She has!' Niki replied, grabbing the swing. Laura

and Sarah joined Niki but Louise hesitated. *This is so boring*, she thought. *I remember when you three were fun, but I don't remember when you turned into such bullies*. Then she noticed that Niki was giving her one of her weird looks. Louise knew the look well. It said, *are you with us or not?*

'What?' she said, staring back at Niki.

'*Nothing*. God, Louise, you can be *so* touchy sometimes,' Niki said, and Louise felt her face redden as Laura and Sarah frowned at her.

Louise opened her mouth to say something, then shut it again. It was no good. If she tried to explain herself, she'd only make it worse. 'I'm just a bit stressed about that maths test we had, that's all,' she lied. Forcing a smile, she grabbed a swing and joined in.

'Girls – over there,' said Sarah. 'Looks like we've got trouble.' Louise watched the girl's mother go marching up to a park attendant and point towards the four of them. *Oh no*, Louise thought. *Nice one, Niki – she'll want our names, and then what school we go to, and all for these stupid swings that we're too old for anyway.*

Niki jumped off. 'We're out of here! That little blabbermouth has told on us.'

The park attendant was gesturing at them and he broke into a run. Louise slowed the swing with her feet, got off and pelted towards the park gates along with the other three. The park attendant gave chase and Niki, Laura and Sarah began to hoot with laughter. Louise couldn't help laughing too as she saw the attendant, who was a chunky, red-faced man with short legs, trying to catch them.

'You girls! Stop right there!' he puffed.

'It's like being chased by a beach-ball!' Laura panted.

As they reached the gates, Louise glanced back to see that the park attendant had given up. Laura and Sarah flopped down on a bench. Louise felt relieved that they weren't going to get caught this time, but that feeling of relief was torn out of her when she saw the little girl from the swings. She was sobbing, clutching her mum's legs. She looked round to see whether Laura and Sarah had seen what they'd done. But they were looking in another direction. They were looking at Niki.

'Well, girls. That brat has just ruined our afternoon's entertainment. Any ideas on who we can wind up next?' she said, a broad grin stretching across her face.

Louise knew what was coming.

'Mr W-W-Webster!' Sarah said.

'Got it in one!' Niki grinned.

Mr Webster owned the sweet shop in the little parade of shops opposite the park gates. Louise thought that 'Webster's Box of Delights' was the most amazing shop she had ever been in. Mr Webster made all the sweets himself in the kitchen at the back of the shop and each one was totally unique and tasted so much better than the mass-produced stuff.

'OK!' Niki said as they reached the shop. 'What's on the menu today?'

'I don't believe it,' Sarah moaned, 'I've only got 20p left!'

'Don't worry about it, Sar,' Niki said, smiling the smile that Louise had grown to distrust. 'Who needs money?'

'What are you like?' Laura laughed.

'Well, he shouldn't charge so much, should he?' Niki cackled.

Louise hated it when her friends got like this. She had known the girls since they were all small, and she knew that none of them *needed* to take anything from shops without paying. But for some reason Niki had started doing it recently, and Laura and Sarah just did it for kicks. Louise wasn't sure about the person that Niki was turning into. 'I've got some cash so I'm going to pay for mine anyway,' she said, trying to make it sound casual.

Niki scowled at her. 'You're no fun, Louise. Why don't you just go home?' There was a vicious edge to her voice.

Louise swallowed hard. She could hear her heart

pounding in her ears. 'I'll go where I want, when I want – you're not my mum, Niki, so just back off.' Louise could feel Laura and Sarah staring at her in disbelief but she refused to let her gaze waver, looking steadily at Niki.

There was a long pause then suddenly Niki gave a big grin. 'That's my girl,' she said, slapping Louise on the back. 'I can always count on you to rise to my jokes!'

How was that a joke? Louise thought angrily. Niki banged through the door, making the bell jangle madly. Louise tried to calm herself down. *I don't have to do anything I don't want to*, she told herself firmly.

Coming into the cool interior of Webster's always felt like travelling back in time. The smell of sweets mixed with the aroma of polish on the ancient wooden counters was like nothing else she had ever known. She loved the way the coloured windowpanes made the light in the shop seem dim and mysterious. The rainbow colours flickered over the shelves with their rows of huge glass jars, full of amazing sweets of every size and shape. They seemed to glow like jewels.

'WEY-HEY, MR WEBSTER! WE'RE HERE!' Niki shouted, shattering the calm of the interior of the shop.

Louise followed Niki, Sarah and Laura over to the curving mahogany counter that took up one side of the shop. She inspected the glass-fronted display of chocolates and sweets, some so special they were individually wrapped and priced.

Mr Webster came shuffling out from the back room in his shabby old slippers. He had a bald head that looked like he polished it, pink speckled cheeks and small eyes that peered at them over his ancient-looking spectacles.

'I knew it was you lot,' he grumbled. 'You're like a herd of wild elephants.' As he stood waiting for them to order, Louise could feel tension rising inside her as she watched Sarah swap the signs on the displays around, right in front of the shopkeeper.

'W-w-what d'you think you're doing?' Mr Webster

spluttered. Louise knew that when Mr Webster got upset or angry, he started to stutter. She felt sorry for him because this was what Niki, Laura and Sarah found funniest of all.

'Just trying to help you, Mr Webster,' Sarah replied, putting on an innocent look. 'I think this one goes here, doesn't it?' She picked up a sign saying 'Mango Surprise' and replaced it with one saying 'Banana Ripple'.

'Leave that alone!' Mr Webster made a grab for the sign. But before he could reach it, Sarah handed it across to Laura.

'Come on, Mr Webster,' Laura said, moving out of his reach. 'Surely you know it's rude to grab.'

Louise watched as Niki leaned over a nearby 'DO NOT TOUCH' notice. She was cramming chocolate into her mouth, appearing not to care whether Mr Webster was watching or not. Louise felt a knot of anxiety uncoiling in her stomach. They really seemed to have it in for Mr Webster.

'Now where can we put this?' Laura said, moving

the sign over to the other side of the shop.

But Mr Webster had spotted Niki. 'Anything y-y-you touch, you'll pay f-for,' he said angrily.

'Pay for what? I haven't touched anything!' Niki replied. 'Prove it, Webster,' she said, flashing him a defiant look.

'You saw her, didn't you?' Mr Webster spun round and faced Louise. 'I bet you've been taking things too.'

'I haven't. Honestly!' Louise replied indignantly.

C-c-can't you read?' Mr Webster said, sweeping past her, heading for Laura. 'It says DO NOT TOUCH.'

'Oh no, I thought it said *DO* TOUCH! Silly me. You really should write your signs better, Mr Webster,' Laura replied.

'B-b-b—' Mr Webster began.

Louise found herself smiling in spite of herself. It was quite a funny sight, with Mr Webster rushing around trying to stop Niki, Laura and Sarah from rearranging his carefully constructed displays.

At that moment, Louise felt something pulling at her side. Looking down, she saw that Niki had stuffed a large handful of foil-wrapped sweets into Louise's jacket pocket. Louise tried to shove them down further so they were out of sight.

'What are you doing?' she hissed at Niki. She could feel her cheeks burning.

'Shut up and go along with it, then we won't get caught,' replied Niki, spitting the words back at Louise.

Louise felt mortified – there was no way she could explain this without either looking like a grass in front of the girls, or like a thief in front of Mr Webster. She hated Niki for putting her in this situation. Louise concentrated as hard as she could. *Don't go red – he'll know you've done something wrong*, she ordered herself.

'So are you buying anything or not?' Mr Webster demanded, staring hard at Louise. She felt Niki nudge her in her side.

'Hmm – I'm not sure. What do you think, Louise?'

Niki said, staring at Louise and smiling a horribly smug smile.

'Nothing today,' she said quickly. 'I was . . . just checking that no one had taken my mobile,' she said, patting her pocket.

'Hey, girls, look at those!' Niki said. She was staring at the top shelf. A small stack of red velvet-covered boxes had been placed on one of the top shelves. Shining satin ribbons trailed from them and curled down over the shelf. And printed in looping gold lettering on the edges of the boxes were the words '*Webster's Specials*'. The boxes looked more beautiful than anything Louise had ever seen in Webster's.

'What's in those, Mr Webster?' Louise asked.

Mr Webster pushed his glasses up his nose. 'Never you mind.'

'But can't we buy some?' asked Niki.

'Certainly not,' Mr Webster snapped. 'They're new, and they're not for you.'

'Why not?' Sarah replied hotly.

13

'Forget it, Sarah.' Niki turned back to Mr Webster. 'Keep your stupid old boxes, then,' she jeered. 'They wouldn't be special enough for us, anyway. Come on, girls.' Laura and Sarah followed her out of the shop. Louise took one more look at the Specials before going out too.

'Those sweets must taste *really* good if they're in boxes like that,' Sarah mused as they trudged down the street. Louise was hardly listening. She was thinking about what Niki had done in the shop. She thrust her hand into her pocket and pushed the stolen sweets into Niki's chest.

'Don't you *ever* do that to me again!' she said. 'If you want to take things, do your own dirty work.'

Niki looked shocked for a second. '*Oooooo* . . .' she smiled. 'Touchy!'

'Yeah – don't scare us, Louise!' Laura teased.

'Don't worry, LouLou,' said Niki, 'I always do my own dirty work.' She pulled out handfuls of sweets from her own pockets. 'I just thought you might like to live on the wild side for once. Guess I was wrong!' she said, rolling her eyes.

It was Friday, and the girls were having a sleepover at Sarah's house. Sarah had rented their favourite film, and her mum had made a really nice-looking chilli con carne. Louise was having a really good time – just four friends laughing about the stupid stuff that goes on at school.

The film was coming to the scene where the girls usually recited all the lines, choosing a part each. Louise was normally the hunky guy, chasing the affections of the blonde.

But something was wrong. Louise looked at Niki, who pushed aside her carton of popcorn with a look of disgust. 'This tastes like cardboard,' she grunted.

Louise could feel the mood in the room change. Laura looked quickly across at Sarah, and wordlessly she walked over and switched off the TV.

'Why wouldn't he sell us those sweets?' Niki said quietly, pretty much to herself. 'They must be *really* exclusive,' she breathed. 'That's why he keeps them out of reach.'

'Maybe he uses the best cocoa beans for the chocolate,' Laura suggested.

'And all the other ingredients come from this top-secret factory,' Sarah said in hushed, dramatic tones.

'Whatever makes them special is going to stay a secret, anyway,' said Louise. 'Those boxes are far too high up for us to get to.'

'Well – if he's not *selling* them,' Niki gave a big grin, 'we'll have to help ourselves.'

'Yesss!' hissed Sarah.

'But how can we get them? They're on the top shelf,' Louise said. She'd hoped the problem of them being so high up would have put Niki off any plan she had.

'We'll have to wait until there aren't any customers,' Niki said. 'Then find some way of getting Mr Webster out the back.'

'That's not going to be easy, is it?' Louise pointed out desperately. She wanted to nip this plan in the bud now, so that Niki would move on to some other idea.

Niki stopped for a second. 'Maybe we could tell him we can smell something burning in his kitchen—'

Laura interrupted her. 'No – what we do, right, one of us calls Mr Webster. I've never seen a telephone in his shop, so I'm betting that it must be in the kitchen . . .'

'Then what? The rest of us sneak in and take the boxes?' Louise watched as Sarah put two and two together in her head.

'You've got it,' Laura replied.

'Sounds good to me,' Niki said. Then she turned to Louise. 'You in?'

Louise thought for a moment. *It's only some stupid sweets. It's not like anyone will get hurt in the process. And Niki's going to make my life hell if I don't.*

'Well?' Niki asked.

Louise took a deep breath. 'I'm in,' she said.

* * *

Louise and the others stood in the entrance to the park, watching the shoppers wandering down the high street.

'OK,' Niki said, her gaze fixed on Webster's shop window. 'Who's going to put in the call to W-Webster?' She turned to look pointedly at Louise. Louise prepared herself to say no, because she was sure that she'd be far too nervous to be a convincing customer.

'Wait – Laura! You're good at voices,' Niki said suddenly, and Louise felt instant relief. No way did she want to have to make that hoax call.

'Cool!' Laura looked really chuffed. 'OK. Here goes. This is the trial run. "Well, hello. Is that Mr Webster? Jolly good. I'd simply love—"'

'Don't go over the top!' Niki hissed at her angrily.

Laura shifted uncomfortably under Niki's glare. 'All right, Niki – sheesh. "Anyway . . . so if you'd just make up the following for me, that would be marvellous. I'd like them put into gift boxes and wrapped in some gold paper. You do *have* gold paper—"'

Niki stopped her, mid-flow. 'OK – that'll do.'

Louise suddenly had a thought. 'What happens when nobody turns up to collect the order?'

Niki let out an overly dramatic sigh. 'Chill *out*, Louise. By the time that the old man realizes what is going on, we'll have got ourselves a couple of boxes of those Specials.'

'Where shall we hide beforehand?' Laura said, scanning the pavement opposite.

'What about behind those?' Sarah pointed at a line of wheelie bins.

'People might see us and wonder what we're doing,' Louise replied.

'Live dangerously for once, Louise!' Niki grinned, shoving her in the arm. Before Louise could respond, Niki ran off towards the shop, barely looking before running across the busy road. In a moment, Sarah followed her, and Louise found that she too was moving faster and faster. She could feel excitement taking the place of nerves, and followed Sarah's lead, barely paying attention to the drivers honking their horns around them. With the blood rushing in her ears, she made it across the two lanes of traffic. A van screamed to a halt right next to her, and the driver hooted furiously and rolled down his window. 'Look where you're going!' he yelled.

'Sorry!' Louise grinned, and looked up to make sure that Mr Webster hadn't seen the commotion, before joining Niki and Sarah down behind the wheelie bins.

Niki was fuming. 'What are you *doing*? You could have blown the whole thing!'

'Bet old Webster saw you.' Sarah tucked a straying blonde curl back under her woolly hat, looking cross. 'He'll be watching out for us now.'

Through the old, coloured windowpanes, Louise could just make out Mr Webster serving a customer. She crouched down beside Niki and Sarah. 'It's OK. He's serving someone. He can't have seen me,' she said.

'This is just like being in a film,' Sarah said.

'I hope it's not *Mission: Impossible*!' Louise whispered back.

'OK, so this is what we're going to do: when Webster goes out back to answer Laura's call, we get in there and find something to stand on. Then we get a couple of boxes of Specials, and get out,' Niki instructed. 'Louise – while me and Sarah get the Specials, you lean against the kitchen door to stop Webster coming out.'

Now all we do is wait for the customer to leave, thought Louise. She could feel a strange mix of excitement and gut-turning anxiety coursing around her body.

'Please don't let anyone else go in,' prayed Sarah.

'Come on. Get out of the shop,' Niki said under her breath.

The couple of minutes they waited for the last customer to leave the shop felt like an hour. The woman walked past the girls carrying a large, gold-wrapped package. Louise, Niki and Sarah did their best to look inconspicuous. Louise stared pointedly at the ground, and Sarah decided to concentrate on her text message inbox.

After a moment, Niki spoke up. 'Right – this is it!

Double-check that she was the last one in, then we can get going.' Louise got up and casually walked past the window. She caught a glimpse of Mr Webster putting a jar back on a shelf. He had his back to her, so she slowed down, making sure that he was really on his own.

'All clear,' she whispered to Niki and Sarah.

Niki signalled to Laura, who was standing ready by the park gates. Louise stayed put on the other side of the shop, just out of view from the inside, and waited for Laura to make the phone call. Sure enough, the noise of a phone ringing came from the back of Mr Webster's shop, and Louise watched as he hurried out the back, closing the door behind him.

'Go!' Niki said, her eyes glinting.

Louise walked over and opened the shop door, and Niki and Sarah went straight in. They could hear Mr Webster's muffled voice talking on the phone and Louise could just make out a few snatches of his conversation.

'. . . of course . . . no trouble at all. Just a moment, I'll get a pencil . . . No, that's wonderful, wonderful . . .'

'Get something to stand on,' Niki whispered to Sarah.

'There! Under the counter.' Sarah had spotted a stool that looked just about tall enough. Louise watched, her blood pounding in her ears, as Niki and Sarah gently lifted the heavy wooden stool and set it down near the old-fashioned shelves on top of which the Specials were stacked.

'Louise – go and see what's going on with Webster,' Niki said, as she gingerly climbed on to the old wooden stool. Louise walked over and leaned close to the large old door that led through to the kitchen. She tried to calm her breathing in case Mr Webster heard.

'So let me get it straight, madam – you'd like thirteen boxes of the . . .'

Louise turned back to Sarah and Niki and gave them a thumbs-up. Niki grinned at her, and managed to haul herself upright on top of the high stool. Sarah stood underneath her, holding her as securely as she could. Louise was glad that it wasn't her up on that stool – it looked a little too unstable for her liking.

Suddenly, Louise heard Mr Webster raise his voice.

'This is all a joke to you, isn't it, young lady?' He was shouting. She'd never heard him this angry before. 'Well, it *isn't* to me. This is my livelihood. I'll find out who you are, don't worry. And then you'll be sorry—'

'He's on to Laura!' Louise hissed to Niki and Sarah. 'Quick – I'll try to hold the door, but we have to go *now*.'

Niki stared at her, frozen, fingertips touching the velvet boxes of Specials.

'*Hurry!*' Louise said urgently, as she leaned against the door as much as she could.

Suddenly, the kitchen door began to rattle.

'Who's out there?' Mr Webster shouted. 'You'll

be sorry – you'd better hope I don't get hold of you . . .'

Louise's excitement was swept away by a torrent of fear and regret. As she jammed her foot at the base of the door, she could feel panic rising within her. *What had she been thinking?* She knew that this was a thoroughly stupid plan, and she felt hot with anger for allowing herself to go along with it.

The door juddered alarmingly. Mr Webster must be throwing his weight against it.

'Niki! I can't hold on! He's—'

At that moment, Louise felt herself being flung away from the door. She landed heavily on one knee, and felt it twist under her weight. The pain was bad, but she immediately forgot it as Mr Webster burst through, looking around wildly. The look in his pale eyes sent a chill right through her.

'What on earth's going on?' he raged. There was no sign of his stutter any more. 'You'll pay for this!' he screamed. As he came towards them, Louise felt terrified.

Everything that followed seemed to happen in slow motion. Niki, fingers clutching at a box of the Specials, lost her balance. Louise watched as the stool tilted beneath her and Niki began to fall. In an attempt to save herself, Niki grabbed at a shelf holding several large glass jars. Her weight tore the entire thing from the wall. The jars came crashing down, and Louise shielded herself as glass exploded and sweets scattered everywhere. Mr Webster seemed so stunned that he was rooted to the spot. There was a second's terrible silence as they all stared, round-eyed, at the destruction around their feet.

'RUN!' shouted Niki.

Louise felt as if someone had pressed a switch inside her. She felt her muscles explode with energy as she headed for the door, desperate to escape. Niki's shout seemed to be the signal for Mr Webster to spring to life too. He was purple with rage, moving faster than she would have ever thought possible.

'Niki – watch out!' Louise shouted.

'Got you, you little vandal!' Mr Webster said triumphantly, as he grabbed Niki by the upper arm and dragged her around to face him.

'Let *go*!' Louise saw Niki struggling frantically to free herself. 'Aargh, get off! That hurts!'

'Why have you done this?' Mr Webster said, shaking her furiously. 'Look at the mess. All I've worked for. Ruined!'

Niki looked terrified. Louise was suddenly very worried about what Mr Webster might be capable of while he was this angry. She charged at the shopkeeper, knocking into his side. In the confusion, Niki managed to free herself and dived under his arm, kicking out at his ankle as she did. Caught off balance, Mr Webster stumbled and crashed over on to the floor. Seizing the moment, heart pounding madly, Louise went racing after Niki, feet crunching in the spilled wreckage as she dived for the door.

Laura was waiting as Niki and Louise came rushing up, and the three of them almost fell through the park gates and into the shrubbery. Louise sat down heavily on the grass, relief washing over her.

'I'll never go near that shop again, never! He grabbed me so hard,' Niki said, pulling up her sleeve to reveal a hand mark. 'It really hurt!'

'But what's happened to Sarah?' Laura asked. 'Where is she?'

Louise and Niki looked at each other.

'She must have been caught,' Louise said, the small feeling of relief disappearing again immediately.

Niki glared at Louise. 'You blew it! It's your fault he's got Sarah.'

Louise felt rage well up in her. 'My fault? It was your stupid plan that got Sarah caught and it's down to me that you didn't get caught too!'

Niki seemed to shrink. After a moment, she broke the silence, staring at the red marks on her arm. 'What an idiot!' she grumbled. 'Look what he's done!'

Louise didn't bother to reply. She scanned the road, half hoping that Sarah had made it out of the shop and that she'd chosen to go home or maybe down the high street.

'I'm going to report him,' Niki scowled. 'There's this law that says if you make a mark that shows up – and this one does 'cos you can almost see his fingerprints – you can be arrested.'

Something in Louise suddenly snapped. 'Oh, right! So who *exactly* are you going to report him to?'

Niki looked up in surprise. 'What?'

'Were you thinking of telling the police, then?' Louise said pointedly.

'No . . . I was just . . .' Niki frowned.

Louise could feel her voice get strong and forceful. ' 'Cos they'd be really interested, wouldn't they?' Louise went on. 'Hmmm – let's see. What would you say? "We were trying to steal stuff and the owner of the shop tried to stop us." ' She smiled grimly. 'Oh, yeah, Mr Webster would be in real trouble, I *don't* think!'

Sullenly, Niki pulled down her sleeve.

'It's OK for you,' she muttered. 'He didn't grab you.'

'But he seems to have grabbed Sarah. She's still in there.'

Niki looked away.

'We have to go back for her,' Louise said. 'We have to say we're sorry to Mr Webster.'

'Sorry? No way!' Niki said, shocked. 'Are you crazy?'

'We might get off more lightly if we do. This was a stupid plan from the start,' Louise said, staring hard at Niki.

Niki looked furious. 'Oh, right! So if it was so dumb, why didn't you say you didn't want to do it?'

Louise was silent for a second. Why *hadn't* she? There'd been so many times when she'd wanted to say what she thought. But each time, she'd chickened out, afraid she wouldn't be one of the group any more.

There was a moment's uncomfortable silence, only punctuated by the noise of cars and motorbikes rushing by on the nearby road.

Suddenly, Laura piped up. 'Louise is right,' she

said to Niki. 'We can't leave Sarah. We have to go back.'

Niki looked shocked. Louise thought it was probably the first time Laura had ever disagreed with her.

'Well, have it your own way,' Niki grumbled. As she spoke, she pulled something out from under her jacket. The other two stared. It was a red velvet box with curling satin ribbons and looping gold letters on the side.

'Oh, wow! Awesome!' Laura said enthusiastically.

Louise stared in disappointment at the sweets laid out inside the box. They looked like the most boring sweets in the world – white and the size and shape of ping-pong balls.

'What's so special about those?' Niki said, taking one out and turning it over.

'What a con – stupid old Webster must have been winding us up!' Laura replied.

Louise frowned. 'It's weird, isn't it? They just look like massive gobstoppers.'

'Maybe they *look* boring but inside they're amazing,' Laura said hopefully.

Louise, Niki and Laura all took a Special and began to suck on it. Louise felt like spitting it out – they were as nasty-tasting as they were boring-looking.

'It tastes like eating paper,' Laura said, mid-mouthful.

'Paper would have been less hassle to get!' Niki said grimly.

Louise crunched down on the Special, and it shattered in her mouth. After a moment's chewing, she said, 'We'd better go back to the shop and find Sarah.' She swallowed hard, and the fragments of the sweet were gone.

'OK,' Niki sighed. Laura gave a little nod as if she didn't trust herself to speak.

As they began to make their way towards Mr Webster's shop, Louise swallowed again. The Special had left a faint, coppery tang in her mouth.

The three girls waited for the traffic lights to

change so they could cross the road. They were in no hurry this time. Mr Webster's shop now looked quite different to Louise – not inviting or exciting at all. As they crossed, Louise noticed that the old beige blinds had been drawn across the window so you couldn't see in.

She was beginning to feel very shaky. Her entire face felt like it was a little sunburned, and at the same time her hands, feet and neck tingled as though she'd been lying in the snow. She definitely wasn't looking forward to seeing Mr Webster again.

They arrived at the shop door. The sign now read 'Closed' but the door was still slightly ajar. Louise turned to Niki and Laura. 'Ready?' she asked.

The other two nodded, not looking ready at all. Louise opened the door and stepped into the shop. In the gloom, she could see Mr Webster, stooped down, slowly brushing the mess into a pile in the corner of the shop. As they entered the shop, he looked up, and Louise braced herself for him to start shouting again. But his expression didn't change. He stared at them for what felt like an age, and then, wordlessly, began to clean up again. There was no surprise in his face at all – it seemed to Louise as if he'd been *expecting* them.

'Did you enjoy the Specials?' Mr Webster asked, not looking up from his task. His voice was steady and quiet, and Louise almost wished he'd shout and rant and leap up and down, rather than stay this calm. It just didn't feel right.

'They were really nice,' Louise lied. She didn't want to risk upsetting him any more than they already had.

'You don't sound very convincing to me,' Mr Webster replied, still not looking up, and still speaking in the same quiet, controlled voice.

Louise could feel her spine stiffening. 'Really, Mr Webster, they were—'

'Sorry, Mr Webster,' Niki interrupted, 'but the truth is that they were a bit of a let-down. It was like having a load of sawdust in your mouth.' Louise looked at her in amazement. That was the last thing they needed – Niki giving him attitude.

'What a shame,' Mr Webster replied. He emptied the contents of his dustpan into a big plastic bag.

'We're really, really sorry, Mr Webster,' Louise said in a rush. 'We shouldn't have taken them in the first place.'

Mr Webster paused, stood up and stared at the three girls. It felt to Louise like he was looking straight through them.

'No, indeed you shouldn't,' he said at last.

'Um . . .' Louise began, 'is our friend Sarah still here?'

'Yes. She's still here. She's in the kitchen helping me to make up for all the damage you've done.' Louise thought she saw a glint in the shopkeeper's eyes.

'Will you be reporting us to the police?' Laura said shakily.

Louise swallowed, but her throat felt really dry. She looked at Niki. The look of defiance from earlier had drained away, along with the colour in her face.

'I'm not going to report you,' he replied. Louise felt relief, even though she was feeling really quite unwell. 'But there is a condition. You've all got to help me too.'

That seems fair, Louise thought. *Just a few hours' work — a bit of stirring and sweeping, and this will all be over.* She turned to see Laura nod and Niki mumble her agreement. They both looked white as sheets.

'OK, Mr Webster,' Louise said. 'We'll give you a hand.'

'Come along, then.' He turned and shuffled off towards the large kitchen door.

As they followed Mr Webster into the kitchen, Louise began to feel really, really weird. Sweat was forming on her forehead and back, and her mouth felt numb — like when she'd gone to the dentist to have a filling. But there was a strange tingling feeling as if someone was sticking tiny pins into her lips. She ran her tongue over them. They were icy cold and it felt as if all the nerves around her mouth were stiffening up. She began to rub her jaw with one hand and press her fingers to her lips with the other. It was odd – the numbness felt even worse than the tingling. She turned her head to see that both Laura and Niki were rubbing their jaws too. She could feel the blood racing behind her eyes, as panic set in.

What was happening?

She dug her fingernails into her lips, desperate to feel something other than the terrifying, frozen nothingness. Frantically, she turned back to Niki and Laura. How could they all be feeling like this? What had they eaten . . .

The Specials!

Her stomach turned over. She felt cold, sick terror swirling inside her.

In the dim light of the kitchen, Louise could see Sarah. She was sitting on a high stool with her back to them, whisking something in a large metal bowl. The whirring and grinding noise of machinery clattered around them. Mr Webster's kitchen seemed less like a kitchen and more like some sort of laboratory.

'Sarah.' Louise managed to move her stiff, numb mouth. Sarah didn't turn round. With a huge effort, Louise shouted even louder. *'Sarah!'* Tentatively, she raised a hand and tapped her friend on the shoulder.

'Sarah—'

Louise froze. Even in the half-light, she could see that Sarah's eyes were dark with terror and her pale cheeks streaked with tears. And then Louise saw why Sarah hadn't answered.

Sarah no longer had a mouth.

Skin covered where it had been. Beneath the skin, Louise watched in horror at Sarah's gums trying to move – to form words – but no sound came out at all, except a thin nasal whine. For all Sarah's frantic efforts, her mouth remained sealed by the terrible, seamless flap of skin.

Louise recoiled, crashing against a high metal table. The invisible clamp on her mouth was tightening and she was becoming dizzy and faint with the pain. She had to get out of this kitchen *now*. She turned around, frantically looking for Niki and Laura. *They all had to get out!*

But as she saw Niki and Laura, the blood in her veins turned to ice. Niki had fallen to her knees, hands tearing madly at her mouth, and Laura was rolling beside her, blue eyes wide and staring in agony.

They no longer had mouths either.

Louise tried to cry out but her teeth felt as though they were welding together. The pain was terrible now, relentless, searing, as if someone was driving a red-hot poker into her jaw.

Welding it shut.

She tried to scream, but the sound came out like the gurgle of water down a drain. Slowly, knowing what she would find, Louise raised her hand to her own mouth – or rather, to the space in her face where her mouth had once been . . .

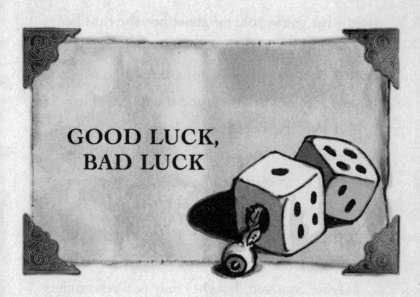

GOOD LUCK, BAD LUCK

'Your gran's not really all there, is she?'

Thirteen-year-old Greg Crowley and his best friend Sam Dee were walking home after school on the Friday afternoon before half-term.

Greg stopped in his tracks at Sam's words and stared at him. Sam was right, his gran was not quite right in her mind – but it wasn't something that he felt comfortable talking about.

Sam gave an apologetic smile. 'Sorry,' he said. 'But

from what you've told me about her, she can't be.'

'She's ill, that's all,' Greg said, frowning as he carried on walking. 'She's got arthritis and she has trouble with her balance – and she forgets things.'

'You said she doesn't even know who you are sometimes when you visit her in that nursing home,' Sam said. Greg could tell he was fascinated by the whole thing.

Greg grimaced. 'OK, so she forgets a *lot* of things,' he said. 'She gets confused and scared. She's old.'

'Maybe,' Sam said, 'but she's only two years older than my gran – and my gran went skiing in Switzerland last year.' He looked at Greg. 'How long has she been in that home?'

Greg thought back. He had no memory of his gran in any other place. His father had told him that years and years ago the nursing home had been a lunatic asylum. Greg found the idea of that a bit creepy.

'It's like she's been there for ever,' he sighed, scratching at his short, spiky brown hair. 'But she wasn't always this bad. We used to take her around the gardens in a wheelchair a few years back. But she doesn't leave her room at all now.' He looked at Sam. His friend's bright blue eyes were sympathetic under his unruly tangle of blond hair.

'That sounds pretty bad,' Sam said.

Greg nodded. 'Her arthritis has got so bad that she hardly ever gets out of bed,' he continued. 'She can't read or knit or do crosswords or puzzles or any of that kind of thing. So she just sits there in bed, watching daytime television for hours on end. And she's got a lot more frightened and confused these days. Sometimes when we visit her she just stares at the walls – I don't know – as if she's seeing things that aren't really there.' He glanced at Sam. 'Things that scare her.'

'What kind of things?' Sam asked.

Greg shrugged. 'I don't know,' he said. 'She looks around the room as if she thinks there are monsters hiding behind the furniture. And she freaks out if you make any sudden noises.'

'How often do you visit her?' Sam asked.

'Two or three times a month,' Greg replied. 'I know this must sound really unkind, Sam – but I wish I didn't have to go. It's totally miserable there. And it's not like Gran gets anything out of it, even when she remembers who we are. And it's got worse since Grandad died.'

Sam looked at him. 'You got on really well with your grandad, didn't you?'

Greg nodded. His grandad had died six weeks ago. It had come completely out of the blue. A heart attack. One minute he had been on the bowling green with his mates, bowling for an easy victory – the next minute he was lying dead on the grass. Just like that.

And the visits to Gran in the nursing home had got worse than ever. Grandad wasn't there to remind Gran who they were. Now she thought they were just a bunch of strangers who came into her room sometimes.

'So, what are we going to do next week?' Sam

asked, breaking into Greg's gloomy thoughts. 'You know – half-term.'

Greg smiled. They had a whole week to themselves.

'I don't know,' he said. 'But I think I deserve some fun after the last few weeks.' He thought for a second. 'I'd like to go to the cinema and there's a new computer game and stuff that I want – but I've spent all my pocket money, so I suppose that's out.'

'I'm flat broke, too,' Sam said. 'We'll just have to find cheap things to do – unless we can come up with some easy way of raising money.'

They were still talking about their plans when they arrived at Greg's front gate.

As they walked up the path, the front door was thrown open and Greg's little sister Edie appeared on the step, her long, centre-parted light-brown hair hanging over her pointy face. She grinned at them.

'I know something you don't!' she said. Then she slammed the front door shut, with both boys still outside.

'Edie?' Greg called. But there was no reply. 'EDIE!'

Greg and Sam looked at one another. 'She's nuts,' Sam said.

Greg didn't have much to do with Edie these days. When he'd been younger, they had played together a lot, but over the past couple of years Greg had outgrown her. After all, when you're out with your mates, the last thing you need is for your little sister to be hanging around. It wasn't fun and it *certainly* wasn't cool.

He fetched the front door key out of his pocket and he and Sam went inside.

'You have to hear that new album I told you about,' Greg said. 'You'll love it – it's really great.'

'It can't be better than their first one,' Sam said. 'Not possible.'

'It is,' said Greg, grinning. 'Trust me. It's brilliant.'

Edie was squatting halfway up the stairs, waiting for them.

'I know something you don't know,' she said.

'You already said that,' Greg responded as he closed

the front door. 'What do you think you know?'

'You'll find out.' Edie turned and scrambled up the stairs and vanished around the corner in a flurry of legs. A moment later there was the bang of her bedroom door closing.

Greg's mother's voice sounded from the kitchen. 'Hey – less noise, please!'

'It was Edie,' Greg called.

'Greg? Aha! You're just the person I want. Come on through, sweetie.'

Sam nudged Greg. 'Sweetie?'

'Shut it,' Greg replied.

His mother's face appeared at the kitchen doorway. 'And Sam, too. That's perfect. How's it going, Sam? Are you feeling fit?'

'I'm fine, thanks, Mrs Crowley,' said Sam, sounding puzzled.

'Great.' She beckoned them in. 'I've got a little proposition to make to the two of you.'

Greg and Sam went through into the sunlit kitchen.

'How do you boys fancy doing a good deed and making a bit of money?' Mrs Crowley asked.

'The money sounds interesting, Mum,' Greg said with a smile. 'But I'm not so sure about the good deed.' He went to the fridge and got out two cans of Coke. 'Good deeds are usually hard work.' He grinned at her. 'What's the plan, then?'

'Grandad's house is going to be sold,' Mrs Crowley said. 'We've arranged for some professional movers to come in and take away all the furniture – but there are a lot of personal things in there that need to be carefully packed up first.' She looked from one to the other. 'So – what do you say? I'll make it worth your while. I know Greg's been keen to get a new computer game – and I bet you've got a long shopping list, too, Sam. How does fifty pounds each sound?'

Sam's eyes lit up and he nodded enthusiastically. 'That sounds very fair to me! What do you reckon, Greg?'

'There you go, Greg,' his mum said. 'Sam's up for it. It'll only take you a couple of days – three at the most. And you'd be helping me and your dad out. We'd do it, but you know your dad has that conference to go to, and I'm busy in the shop.'

Greg's father ran a company that organized large-scale meetings and conferences all over the country. It meant he had to be away from home a lot. His mum owned a flower shop that was open seven days a week, and now that summer was coming she had to be there nearly every day.

Working over in Grandad's house certainly hadn't been one of the things he'd planned for that week – but the money sounded good, and if they worked really fast he and Sam might be able to get it done in a day or so.

'You'll have to explain exactly what you want us to do,' Greg said to his mum.

'I've already made you a list,' she said. 'A load of cardboard boxes are being delivered there in the morning. All you have to do is to fill them up and write on the outside in felt-tip so we know what's in each one.'

'OK,' Greg said. 'When do you want us to start?'

'Tomorrow would be great,' Greg's mum replied. 'The removals men are coming to take the furniture away on Tuesday – and I really want all your grandad's personal stuff gone by then.'

'You up for doing it tomorrow?' Greg asked Sam.

'Why not?'

Greg grinned at his mother. 'Do we get paid up front?'

She laughed. 'You can have some pizza money now – and the rest when you've finished.'

'Excellent.' He looked at Sam. 'Let's go up to my room,' he said. 'There are a couple of tracks on the new album that are going to totally blow your mind.'

They left the kitchen and headed upstairs.

'Did your grandad have a lot of stuff?' Sam asked.

'Not tons,' Greg said. 'There are loads of rooms, but he only lived in about three or four of them. It's a really old house, so you never know – we might even find some interesting stuff. You know, like you get on those antiques programmes on TV – family heirlooms worth thousands of pounds.'

'Do I get a share if we do?' Sam asked.

'Fifty-fifty,' Greg laughed. *Clearing out Grandad's things might actually turn out to be OK*, he thought. He didn't say it out loud, but he also hoped that spending time in the old house might somehow help him come to terms with losing his grandfather. He hadn't been there since the family and friends had met up for a bite to eat after the funeral a month ago. And that had been really grim.

They were halfway up the stairs when Greg's mother appeared in the hallway.

'Oh, I forgot to mention,' she said. 'Edie will be helping you as well. So I want you to keep an eye on her and make sure she doesn't do anything daft. And when you go for food, take her with you, please. She won't be any trouble – she's promised to behave herself and to do what she's told.'

And with that, she went back into the kitchen.

Greg and Sam looked at one another in horror.

'I don't believe it,' Sam said. 'Your mum's set us up.'

From the landing above them, they heard the sound of Edie's bedroom door open. There was a crow of laughter like fingernails down a blackboard – then the door slammed shut again.

Now they knew what Edie had meant when she had said she knew something they didn't.

This was going to be a total nightmare.

'Now then, Edie, listen to me,' said Mrs Crowley, bending down to look square into her daughter's eyes. 'I want you to behave yourself and do what your brother tells you, OK?'

'Yes, Mum,' Edie replied.

Greg, Sam and Edie were standing on the pavement outside the wide wrought-iron gate of Grandad's house.

'And don't race around like a mad thing, and *please* try not to break anything.' She turned to Greg and Sam. 'And remember – pack heavy things at the bottom and the fragile things on the top, right?'

'Of course, Mum,' Greg replied.

His mum smiled. 'Look after her.'

Greg nodded.

'Greg's in charge,' his mum said as she started up the car engine. 'Remember that, Edie!'

'Yes, Mum,' Edie said meekly.

'Bye, then,' Mrs Crowley said. 'You've got my mobile number if there are any problems – and you can contact me at the shop till twelve, OK? And I'll be over this afternoon to see how you're getting along.'

She drove along the curved, tree-shaded road and was gone.

Greg turned to his sister. 'You're going to do what I tell you, right?' he said firmly.

She gave him a withering look. 'In your dreams,' she said.

'Edie!'

'You're not my boss,' she said, pushing the gate open. 'Where are the keys?'

'In my pocket.'

'Give them to me.'

'No.'

Edie glared at him. She took out her mobile phone. 'Give them to me *right now* or I'll call Mum and tell her you're being a total pig to me.'

Greg took the keys out of his pocket and dropped them into her hand. 'Fine,' he said. 'Have them. What do I care? Just keep out of our way, all right?'

Edie went racing up the crazy-paved path between the rhododendron bushes.

'Way to keep her under control,' Sam said, laughing.

'Trust me on this,' Greg said. 'It's going to be easier if we just let her do what she wants. If we try to tell her what to do, it'll turn into a war. With any luck, she'll go off somewhere and spend the morning chatting to her dopey friends on her mobile.'

'Just so long as she doesn't invite them over,' Sam said.

Greg stared at him in alarm. 'Don't even *think* that!' he said.

They walked up the path. The big old green-painted door was wide open on to the familiar hallway. But Greg could see that there were already less familiar things in there.

The hallway was stacked with flat-packed piles of cardboard boxes and reels of brown tape, and rolls of white wrapping-paper stood nearby.

'Smells a bit funny in here,' Sam said, still standing on the doormat.

Greg walked into the hallway. 'This is the way it always smells,' he said.

It gave Greg a strange, hollow feeling to look at his grandad's things again. All he remembered about the last visit to the house after the funeral was being totally miserable, and wishing Grandad had been there to say something funny and make him laugh.

But there was no Grandad here to tell funny stories. There was just a big old empty house full of stuff that didn't belong to anyone any more.

Greg looked around at his grandad's things. The old upright piano that no one played. The two-seater couch with the wickerwork back and the seat covers with the huge red flowers on them. The leather footstool. The big old table with the four chairs. And the faded and worn leather armchair he used to sit in.

'This is just like a museum,' Sam said, gazing around.

'My mum said that Grandad didn't change anything after Gran went into the home. He left it all like this so he'd remember her better, I suppose – something like that.'

'Old people do strange stuff sometimes,' Sam said. He glanced at Greg. 'Sorry – I didn't mean your grandad was strange.'

'He wasn't,' Greg said, more sharply than he meant. 'He just missed Gran.'

Sam homed in on an ancient stereogram with a black Perspex lid. There were boxes of vinyl LPs nearby.

'Wow! State-of-the-art hi-fi!' Sam said with a grin. He lifted the lid. 'There's even a turntable.' He looked at Greg. 'What kind of music did he listen to? Classical stuff or what?'

'Take a look for yourself,' Greg said, nodding towards the row of boxes along the wall. 'They're alphabetical.'

Sam opened one of the boxes and pulled an LP out. ' "Manuel and his Music of the Mountains",' he read from a cover that showed a picture of snow-capped mountains. 'I bet it's killer.' He pulled out more albums. 'James Last? Mantovani? Herb Alpert.' He shook his head. 'I've never heard of *any* of these people.'

'Beethoven's *Pastoral Symphony*,' Greg read. 'There you go – you must have heard of Beethoven.'

'I bet he doesn't get downloaded too often,' Sam chuckled. 'Let's play something – just for a laugh.'

Greg felt a twinge of disloyalty to Grandad, watching Sam making fun of his music like that, but he slid an LP out of its cover and put it on the turntable. He switched the hi-fi on and moments later a scratchy noise came out of the speakers –

followed by a blast of big-band music.

Sam stood up, grinning from ear to ear. 'That's really bad,' he laughed.

'True,' Greg admitted, smiling in spite of himself. 'Old people have such weird taste in music.'

Greg leaned over the hi-fi and switched it off. He watched as the needle arm lifted. The scratchy music stopped. Greg stood up. 'Come on – we need to get going or we'll be here all week.'

They went out into the hall and dragged a pile of flat boxes through into the living-room. Sam assembled them and Greg secured the bottoms with the brown tape. Soon they had quite a pile ready to be packed.

'Where's your sister gone?' Sam asked.

'Don't know. Don't care,' Greg said. 'Just so long as she keeps out of our way, she can do what she likes. OK – where do we start?'

'Heavy stuff at the bottom,' Sam said. He walked over to the piano and picked up a statuette of an elephant. 'This is pretty heavy.'

'OK, wrap it in the paper and stick it in the box,' Greg said.

'It's all dusty and filthy,' Sam said with a grimace. 'Everything's covered in dust. And there's cobwebs and all sorts down the back of this piano.'

'Don't look,' Greg said. 'Just think of the money.'

A loud crash from directly above made them both jump.

Greg stared up at the ceiling. 'Oh, no! Edie!' he groaned.

'You *were* told to keep an eye on her,' Sam said helpfully.

Greg gave him an exasperated look. 'We'd better go and see what's she's done.'

They headed up the stairs and around on to the landing. One door was open at the far end – the door of the room directly above the living-room.

'Edie?' Greg shouted. 'What are you doing?'

'It wasn't my fault,' came Edie's voice from inside the room. 'It just fell.'

Edie was in a big room with a pale red carpet and

59

floral wallpaper. There was a big double bed with a rose-patterned covering. Two bedside tables. A dressing-table with three mirrors. A chest of drawers. Two big wardrobes. It smelled as if there had been no heating in there for a very long time.

Greg immediately saw what had smashed. A full-length mirror on a polished wooden stand lay face down on the carpet. Shards of glass were scattered across the floor. Edie was standing as far away from it as possible, her face sullen and defiant. 'It fell over,' she said.

'On its own, I bet,' said Greg sarcastically. 'What were you doing?'

'Nothing,' Edie said. 'It's *not* my fault.'

'That's seven years' bad luck,' Sam said, peering over Greg's shoulder. 'Breaking a mirror.'

'It's not!' Edie said. 'Anyway – I didn't break it. It fell over.'

The fallen mirror was in front of one of the wardrobes. Ranged along the top of the wardrobe were a group of dolls with porcelain faces and old-fashioned clothes. One doll was missing from the row. It was lying face down on the carpet.

'You were climbing on it to try and get at the dolls, weren't you?' Greg said.

'No.'

'You're such a liar, Edie,' Greg said. 'Go and see if you can find a dustpan and brush in the kitchen.'

Edie shoved past them and hammered her way down the stairs.

'Great,' Greg sighed. 'Mum will do her nut when she sees this. And it's probably a really valuable antique or something. That girl is a total disaster area.'

Between them, Greg and Sam managed to lift the mirror in its heavy wooden frame. Only the top part of the mirror was actually shattered – the rest of it was still held in the frame. They picked up the fragments of glass and put them together in the hearth of the fireplace.

'Where is your sister with that dustpan and brush?' Sam asked.

'Oh, she's probably off somewhere having a sulk,' Greg said. 'But it doesn't matter – guess who'll get the blame?'

Sam opened the door to the wardrobe that had been covered by the mirror.

'That was Gran's wardrobe,' Greg said.

'There's something in the bottom here,' Sam said. He leaned in and brought the thing out.

Greg went over to look.

It was a sheet of thick card, folded in two and hinged with some green tape.

'What is it?' Greg asked. 'It looks like some kind of game board – you know, like for Monopoly or something.'

Sam crouched on the carpet and carefully opened the thing. 'I don't think so,' he said. 'I think it's a map.'

Greg knelt at his side, leaning close to have a better look.

The map was amazingly detailed and beautifully drawn in colours that had faded over the years. Woods and open land were picked out in greens;

roads and paths in yellows and greys; buildings in soft red tints or in shades of brown.

In a flowing script all around the map, the same phrase was repeated over and over again: **Make Your Own Luck. Make Your Own Luck. Make Your Own Luck.**

'Oh, wow!' Greg breathed. 'It's not just a map – it's a map of *here*.' He pointed to a green space. 'Look – that's the park – and there's St Matthew's Church. And the high street.' But there were things that were different – and things that were missing as well. 'Where's our school?' he wondered aloud.

'The shopping centre's not there either,' said Sam. 'Nor is the multistorey car park.'

'Hey, you know what this is, don't you?' Greg said. 'It's a map of how the town looked in the past.' He leaned in even closer. 'Look! It's got this house on it.'

Sure enough, there it was on the map; except that on the map there was no park next to it – there was just open woodland.

Greg traced his finger along the path which led

from the main part of the town, through the woods and right up to the front door of Grandad and Gran's house. But it was not quite like the other roads and tracks shown on the map. It was divided into squares, and for some reason, the mapmaker had given each square its own particular colour. Greg followed the path to the house. It ended at the front door. Written on the doorstep was the word 'START'.

Sam looked closely at the coloured path. 'There are tiny little things drawn on it,' he said. 'See? There's a different one on each square. Weird.'

'There's writing on some of the squares, too,' Greg said. 'You know what this is, don't you? It *is* a board game! Is there anything else in the wardrobe? Instructions or anything?'

Sam delved into the wardrobe again. 'Yes!' he said.

It was a small wooden box with a sliding lid. A piece of paper had been glued on to the lid and on it, in old-fashioned, faded ornate lettering, were the words 'GOOD LUCK, BAD LUCK'.

Inside the box was a pack of yellowing playing-cards held together by a piece of knotted ribbon. There was also a pair of dice, a small wooden cup and a tatty booklet. Sam lifted the booklet out of the box. 'Hey, look at these,' he said. Underneath lay two little wooden figures.

Greg picked the two figures out and stood them up on the board. They were roughly human-shaped, but without much detail. The body of one showed small patches of blue paint – the other had once been painted red. The faces were totally blank – there were no features at all.

'I think all this stuff is handmade and hand-painted,' Greg said, twisting one of the figures in his fingers. He picked up the booklet and opened it. There seemed to be instructions and rules written out inside – but they were written by hand in ink that had faded so much it was lilac-coloured on the browned pages.

'Do you think your gran or grandad might have made it?' Sam asked. 'You know – when they were kids, maybe?'

'It's possible, I suppose,' Greg said. 'I don't know that Gran has ever been artistic like that – but Grandad used to be a jeweller, so he'd be able to do fiddly stuff like the writing on those little squares, I suppose.' He frowned. 'But why didn't he ever show it to me? I'd be really proud if I'd come up with something like that.'

Each square had its own tiny painted object on it. A horseshoe. A pair of magpies. A ladder. A clover leaf. A knife. A crescent moon. A well. A rabbit. A gold ring. A frog. A goblet. A five-pointed star. And every now and then, there was a yellowish square with tiny words written on it: 'Draw a card'.

'Well, the rules seem pretty straightforward,' Sam said. 'There's a lot of detailed stuff, but basically, you start at the house and throw the dice. Whatever number comes up, that's how many squares you move. If you land on one of the yellow squares, you have to pick a card from the top of the deck.' He looked at Greg. 'There's not much to it, is there?'

'Doesn't it say anything about what the drawings

on the squares mean?' Greg asked.

'I'm not sure. Some of the writing is a bit tricky to read.'

Greg picked up the pack of cards. The knot on the ribbon wouldn't come loose, so he carefully eased the cards out of the stiff loop. Written on the back of each card were the words: 'Do you feel lucky?'

Greg was about to turn the top card over to see what was written on the underside when Sam's hand came down on his to stop him. 'No you don't,' Sam said. 'The rules specifically forbid any player from looking at the cards in advance.' He nodded towards the rule book. 'And it says that players have to pay a forfeit if they break any of the rules.'

'Technically, I'm not playing yet,' Greg said.

'Well, that's not exactly true,' Sam said with a wide grin. 'Look – it says right here on the first page that the game begins when the board is opened up.' He laughed. 'Whether you like it or not, we're already playing.'

'So let's play,' Greg said.

There was the stamp of feet on the landing.

'Edie,' Greg groaned. For someone who was all skin and bone, his sister certainly had a loud way of letting you know she was around. 'If she sees us with this game, she'll want to join in.'

'So, let her,' said Sam. 'What's the problem?'

'Edie is a total monster with board games,' Greg said. 'She always cheats and she sulks like mad if she doesn't win. This is *really* old – like, kind of an antique, right? If Edie gets her hands on it she'll probably wreck it.'

'Tell her to get lost, then,' Sam suggested.

'Oh, sure – *that'll* work!' Greg replied. 'Hang on, though – there's a bolt on the door!' He ran across the room and shot the bolt home. A moment later, the door handle rattled.

'Open this door!' Edie shouted.

'No. Go away,' Greg replied. Sam stifled a laugh.

The handle rattled furiously. 'Let me in! Why's the door locked? What are you doing in there?'

'Nothing,' Greg called. 'We're clearing up the glass

from the broken mirror. Push off, Edie. You've made enough trouble. You're not coming in.'

The door shook as Edie kicked it. 'I'm telling Mum on you!'

'Go ahead,' Greg called. 'And I'll tell her about the mirror you broke!'

'Pig!' There was the angry stamp of feet moving away along the landing. Greg and Sam looked at each other and grinned.

'That's got rid of her,' Greg said, kneeling down by the board. 'OK – you start.'

Sam picked up the dice and put them in the little wooden cup. He shook them for a few moments then let them spill out on to the board. 'Three and two,' he said. 'That's five. I'll be blue.' He picked up the wooden figure and walked it down five squares of the path from the house. 'I've landed on a horseshoe.' He frowned. 'Is that good luck or bad luck? I can't remember.'

'I'm pretty sure it's good luck,' Greg said.

Sam smiled. 'Excellent.'

Greg frowned. 'Is there anything in the rules about what actually *happens* when you land on a good-luck square? Do you get an extra turn or something?'

'I don't think so,' Sam said. He handed Greg the booklet. 'You read it.'

Greg flicked through the pages. 'Maybe we should do this later,' he said. He looked at his watch. 'We've been here nearly an hour and we haven't packed up a single thing. Mum will go mad if we don't get busy.'

'What about the game?' Sam asked.

'Just leave it here for now.'

They got up and Greg unbolted the door. They made their way downstairs to the living-room. Edie was stretched out on the couch chattering on her mobile phone.

'You're supposed to be helping!' Greg said to her.

'Just a sec, Rosie,' Edie said into the phone. She glared at Greg. 'I'm talking to my friend,' she said. 'You are *so* rude!'

'Let's just work around her,' Sam suggested.

'If you're not going to be helpful, can you just go somewhere else?' Greg said to Edie.

With irritating slowness, Edie got up off the couch and slouched out of the room, talking on the phone all the while.

'And don't bust anything else!' Greg called after her.

For the next hour or so, Greg and Sam worked quickly and methodically. They wrapped the heavier things and placed them in the bottom of the boxes, then they used scrunched-up paper to make a bedding for the next layer of stuff. The boxes gradually filled and were taped down and labelled with the felt-tip pen. 'Living-Room. Ornaments off the mantelpiece.' 'Living-Room. Framed photos.'

Sam was standing on a chair to reach ornaments on the top shelf of the bookcase when he let out a low whistle.

'What?' Greg asked. He was hot and dusty and sweaty.

'Look at what I found!' Sam said. He turned,

waving a ten-pound note. 'It was in this.' In his other hand he held a shiny china mug with a red horseshoe painted on the side.

'Well, lucky you,' said a voice from the door. They both turned. Greg's mother stood there smiling. 'You boys have been busy,' she said. 'I'm impressed.'

'What time is it?' Greg asked.

'Half past one.'

The time had raced by – Greg had no idea it was so late. Sam climbed down off the chair and held out the ten-pound note to Greg's mother.

She smiled. 'No – you found it, Sam. You can keep it,' she said.

A huge grin spread over Sam's face. 'Thanks, Mrs Crowley,' he said. He looked at Greg. 'That horseshoe did give me good luck after all,' he said.

'What horseshoe?' Greg's mum asked.

'We found a game – Gran and Grandad's board game,' Greg explained. 'The one with the map of our town and everything.'

Mrs Crowley frowned. 'I don't know what you mean, Greg.'

'It's upstairs – I'll go and get it.'

'I'll go up with you,' said his mother. 'I wanted to take a look around the bedroom – there might be a few things I'd like as keepsakes. Gran had a wonderful collection of antique dolls. They're certainly not going to any charity shop.'

Greg looked uneasily at her. 'There's been a bit of an accident,' he said. 'There was a big mirror – on a stand . . . it got broken.'

'Oh, that's a shame,' said his mother. 'But it's my fault – I should have told you to leave the bedroom till I arrived. The frame for that mirror has always been a bit rickety. I hope no one got hurt.' She looked around. 'Where's Edie?' she asked.

'She's around somewhere,' Greg said. 'Last time I saw her, she was chatting on her mobile.'

Greg's mum tutted. 'I told your father giving her a phone of her own was a bad idea,' she said. She looked at them. 'OK, show me this game you mentioned – and then maybe we can all drive to town for some food before we start work again.'

They went up to the bedroom. Mrs Crowley's eyes widened as she caught sight of the game. 'What a fabulous thing,' she breathed, as she knelt down on the carpet and gazed at the board. 'I've never seen it before. I wonder where it's from. I've seen old maps of the local area. This must have been made at least a hundred years ago. And look at all the detail! It's beautiful!'

'I know,' Greg said. 'And it all looks handmade, too.'

'I'm the blue piece,' Sam said, pointing at the figure that was still standing on the board. 'See? I landed on the square with the horseshoe on it. And then I went downstairs and found a tenner in that mug with the horseshoe on it.'

'That's quite a coincidence,' Mrs Crowley said, smiling. Her eyes twinkled as she looked at him. 'Or is it, I wonder?'

'You've *got* to be kidding,' said Greg, exasperated.

'You don't really think this game had anything to do with it, do you?'

His mother laughed. 'No, of course not.' She got up. 'But it's a lovely thing – we should definitely keep it. What say you pack it all up carefully now and put it back into the wardrobe for safe-keeping for the time being. I'll have to ask Gran about it next time we go over there.' She looked at the two friends. 'OK,' she said. 'I think it's time the workers had a lunch break. Let's go down and find Edie, and then get ourselves something to eat.'

'Sam can pay for it with that tenner,' Greg laughed.

'Hey!' Sam said. 'No way!'

'Don't worry, Sam,' Mrs Crowley said, putting her arm around his shoulders. 'I'm paying. You keep that ten pounds. After all, it was your good luck that you found it.'

After lunch, Greg's mum drove them all back to the house for a few more hours' work. Mrs Crowley took

Edie with her upstairs, leaving the two boys to finish packing up the living-room.

'At least she'll have to do some actual work, now,' Greg said as he watched Edie follow his mother up the stairs.

Greg and Sam carried the filled and labelled boxes out and piled them along one wall in the wide hallway.

'Mum?' Greg called up the stairs. 'What's next?'

'I'm just coming,' his mother called.

She came down the stairs carrying a box in her arms.

'I've got all of Gran's dolls, and I'm going to take them home,' Greg's mum said. 'Edie's coming with me – I think she's had enough for today. Haven't you, honey?'

'Yes, Mum.' Edie gave Greg a look of triumph. 'I've been really helpful, haven't I?'

'Yes, you have, sweetie,' her mother said.

'She didn't lift a finger this morning,' Greg protested.

His mother looked at him. 'Well, whose fault is that?' she said cheerfully. 'I left you in charge of her.'

Greg knew there was no point in arguing about it. The more angry he got, the more Edie would gloat.

'Are we all finished for the day, then?' Greg asked.

'I think so,' said his mother. 'I'll tell you what, how about the two of you take a look at what needs doing in the kitchen while I drive Edie over to Rosie's house. Then I'll come back for you and we'll call it a day.'

Sam and Greg helped Mrs Crowley slide the big box of dolls on to the back seat of the car while Edie clambered into the passenger seat. As they drove off, Edie stuck her tongue out at Greg and Sam through the open window.

'I really wish I had a little sister,' Sam said with a fake sigh and a wide grin. 'It must be *so* great.'

'Have mine,' Greg said as they turned to go back

into the house. 'I'll sell her to you for that tenner you found.'

'Not a chance,' Sam said with a laugh. 'But wasn't that amazing, though? Finding the money like that – and in a mug with a horseshoe on it, too. Talk about creepsville.'

'It's not creepsville at all,' Greg said. 'It was just a coincidence.'

'Pete says you should always keep an open mind about stuff like that,' Sam said. Pete was Sam's seventeen-year-old brother.

'I wouldn't pay too much attention to what Pete has to say,' said Greg. 'His mind is so open that his brain keeps falling out.'

'Oh, ha ha,' said Sam. 'All the same – I'm going to do an experiment with that game. I'm going to find out if landing on a lucky square really does work.' He ran along the hall and bounded up the stairs two at a time.

'Hey – what's the idea?' Greg called.

'I'm taking another turn!' Sam said.

Greg chased up the stairs after him.

He found Sam standing in the bedroom doorway, staring at the floor over by the wardrobe.

'That's weird,' Sam said.

'What?'

'Look!' Greg peered over Sam's shoulder. They had tidied the game away back into the bottom of the wardrobe.

But it was out again.

Sam's blue man was back on the board – standing in the horseshoe square. Beside the board, the wooden cup waited with the two dice in it.

'Mum and Edie must have taken it out again,' Greg said.

'And set it up exactly the same as it was?' Sam said, a questioning tone in his voice.

Greg shrugged and pushed past him. 'It's not your turn, don't forget,' Greg said. 'It's mine.'

'It would be if we were playing properly,' Sam pointed out. 'But we're not.' He scooped up the wooden cup.

'Ow!' he exclaimed, dropping the cup immediately. Greg saw that by some fluke it had landed upright on the carpet with the two dice still inside it. Sam sucked his finger.

'What's up?' Greg asked.

'I got a splinter, I think,' Sam said.

'Serves you right,' smiled Greg. He picked up the cup and looked carefully at it. 'But I don't see how,' he said. 'It's completely smooth.'

'I'm telling you that it was a splinter,' Sam complained. 'Look.' He showed Greg his finger. There was a bead of blood on the end. 'Perhaps it was payback for trying to play out of turn,' he grinned. 'Maybe the game doesn't like it when people don't obey the rules.'

'Oh, please!' Greg said with a laugh. 'It's just a board game.'

'It's your turn,' Sam said. 'Roll the dice.'

He tipped the cup and the dice rolled out over the board. 'Ten,' he said. 'Not bad – it beats you, anyway.' He took the red man out of the box and walked it ten squares from the house.

He looked closely at the picture on the square where he had landed.

'It's a ladder,' he said. 'And there's someone falling off it.'

'That's got to be a bad-luck square,' Sam said with a frown. 'You'd better keep well away from ladders for a while.'

'You're a total nutcase, do you know that?' Greg said. 'There's no way that this game could give you good or bad luck. It doesn't make sense.' He put the dice back into the cup. 'Anyway, it's your turn.'

'No thanks,' Sam said. 'Not until I'm sure you're not going to fall off a ladder. I don't want to risk it.'

Greg laughed. 'I can't believe you're being such an idiot about this,' he said.

Sam just shook his head, his face unsmiling.

'Oh, suit yourself,' said Greg. 'Let's pack it away and go and take a look at the kitchen.'

They carefully stowed the game away in the bottom of the wardrobe and headed back downstairs.

All they had time to do in the kitchen before Greg's mum arrived was to make up a few boxes.

'At this rate you'll be finished tomorrow,' she said. 'It's not so bad, is it?' She peered out through the kitchen window into the garden. 'It's a bit of a wilderness out there. I might get someone in to tidy it up a bit before people start viewing the place.' She ran a finger across the pane, leaving a clear trail in the fine dust. 'And these windows could do with a clean.' She looked at Greg. 'Your grandad kept a stepladder in the cellar. Would you mind fetching it up tomorrow and giving the windows a quick shine?'

Greg could see that Sam was staring at him. He turned to his mother. 'A stepladder?' he said uneasily, in spite of himself.

'Yes. You won't be able to reach otherwise,' said his mother. 'But I'm quite happy to do it myself if you don't fancy it.'

'Uh . . . no,' Greg said. 'It's not a problem. I'll do it.'

No way was he going to allow Sam to freak him

out about that game. And no way in the world was he going to fall off that stepladder tomorrow.

Things like that just *didn't* happen.

Greg and Sam had their evening nicely planned out: a Chinese takeaway and a DVD rental to watch at Sam's place. His parents were going out for the evening – his older brother Pete would be in the house but, knowing Pete, he'd be up in his attic bedroom, busy with his PC – which meant they'd have the run of the living-room and the use of the widescreen TV.

It was just beginning to get dark as Greg and Sam cycled along the high street. They propped their bikes against the wall outside the Chinese takeaway and went in to give their order. While the food was being prepared, they headed across the street.

'What movie do you fancy?' Greg asked as they browsed the shelves.

'*Slash and Burn* is meant to be really good,' Sam

said. 'Pete's watched it and he says it's great. But I can't see it here. I'll go and ask.'

They trooped off to the counter.

'You're in luck,' said the assistant, reaching under the counter and bringing out a DVD. 'It was just returned. All the other copies are out right now. It's our most popular movie this week.'

Sam grinned at Greg as he handed over the rental money. 'See?' he said. '*My* luck is still holding out.'

Greg laughed. 'Yeah – right.'

They went back to the takeaway. They had to wait for a few minutes before their order was ready. The woman handed them the carrier bag over the counter and they walked out.

'I'm sure there's more in here than we ordered,' Sam murmured as they came out on to the street. He held the carrier open. 'Yes – there is. Look, it's written on the lids – there's a whole extra special rice, and a carton of sweet and sour pork.' He looked at Greg. 'Wow! Isn't that amazing? Two things we didn't pay for.'

Greg stared into the carrier bag. This was getting weird. Unless Sam's run of good luck ended pretty soon, Greg was going to start wondering about that Good Luck, Bad Luck game.

He moved towards where they had left their bikes. 'I just hope some of your luck rubs off on me,' he said, his head turned over his shoulder towards Sam.

'Hey! Watch out there!'

The voice from above startled him. He turned his head just in time to see the edge of a metal ladder looming right in front of his eyes.

For a moment or two he saw stars. A fierce pain shot through his head and he staggered backwards and fell against the wall.

Dazed and hurt, Greg was vaguely aware of the sound of someone coming down the ladder. 'You could have had me over!' said the voice. 'Why don't you watch where you're going?' The tone of the voice changed to concern. 'Have you hurt yourself?'

Greg had his hand to his head. He blinked at the man standing over him.

'What?' he gasped.

'Are you OK?' asked the man.

Greg noticed that Sam was staring at him with his mouth half open.

'Yes,' Greg said, pulling himself together. 'I'm fine.' He stared at the ladder. Where had that come from? It hadn't been there when they'd gone into the Chinese takeaway.

'That's a stupid place to put a ladder,' he mumbled.

'What?' The man stared at him. 'I can't put up a ladder in front of my own shop to replace a light bulb?'

Sam looked at Greg. 'Are you all right?' he asked. 'You really whacked it.'

Greg blinked at him. 'Is there blood?'

Sam peered close. 'No,' he said. 'But there'll be a massive bruise, I bet.'

'Stupid ladder!' Greg said.

Sam stared at him with an uneasy look on his face.

'What?' Greg said.

'The ladder!' Sam said. 'Don't you get it?'

'Yes, I got it,' Greg said. 'Right between the eyes.'

'No! The *game*!' said Sam. 'The square you landed on had a picture of a ladder on it . . . And you've just walked into a ladder!'

Greg looked at him. 'For a start,' he said, 'the picture was of someone falling *off* a ladder – and no one fell off the ladder. And for a finish, the idea that I walked into a ladder because I landed on that particular square on the board is just completely and utterly ridiculous.' He gave his sore forehead a final rub. 'Come on, let's get back to your place before the food gets cold.'

He grabbed his bike by the handlebars and wheeled it to the kerb. Sam was still standing there staring at him.

'Don't you think it's creepy?' Sam said. 'I landed on a good-luck square and I've had good luck all day – and you landed on a bad-luck square with a ladder on it, and you've just brained yourself on a ladder.' Sam's eyes narrowed. 'Isn't that just a *bit* weird?'

'No,' Greg said, refusing to be drawn into Sam's little fantasy. 'I think *you're* the one who's weird. Get your bike. I'm hungry.'

'OK, have it your own way,' Sam said, hooking the carrier over the handlebars of his bike. 'But if I were you, I wouldn't go climbing any stepladders to wash windows tomorrow.' He shook his head. 'Absolutely no way!'

'Will you just shut up about it?' Greg said, losing his temper a little with his friend. 'I am *never* going to believe that stupid game is giving us good luck and bad luck. It's complete rubbish!'

He didn't believe for one moment that the old board game could have some creepy power to influence a person's life. It was crazy. Impossible.

The next morning, when Greg and Sam and Mum and Edie arrived at Grandad's house, Greg decided that perhaps he didn't feel like washing the windows after all.

'No problem,' Sam said. 'I'll do it.'

He fetched the stepladder out of the cellar and got busy with a bucket and a cloth, cleaning the windows in the front porch.

Greg lugged a bunch of flat-packed boxes and some paper and tape up on to the landing. He was going to make a start on the bedroom.

He opened the door and carried the unmade boxes in and dumped them on the large double bed. He was just about to turn and get the reels of tape and the wrapping-paper when he saw something that stopped him dead in his tracks.

The board game was out. Set up exactly the way it had been yesterday – with the blue figure and the red figure standing in the same places.

'What's going on here?' he murmured. 'How did this get out again?' His eyes narrowed in alarm for a moment then he gave a breath of laughter as he realized what must have happened.

'Oh, very funny, Sam!' he said. 'You are such a comedian!'

Greg bounded down the stairs and ran along the hall. The front door was open and the lower half of Sam was visible as he washed the higher panes of glass in the porch.

'Really funny,' Greg said. 'Ha, ha, ha. I ought to tip *you* off that ladder.'

Sam doubled over and peered at him. 'What are you talking about?'

'The game, dummy,' Greg said. 'Did you think I was going to believe it had set itself up overnight? How stupid do you think I am?'

Sam looked at him. 'Which question do you want me to answer first?' he said. He threw the cloth into the bucket.

'Oh, stop it,' Greg said. 'I *know* it was you. Who else could have done it?'

Sam frowned. 'Are you trying to tell me that the game is out again?' he said.

'You know it is!' Greg replied pointedly.

Sam shook his head. 'I didn't put it out.'

'Oh, give it up, Sam – it didn't scare me for an instant.'

'I haven't even been up there!' Sam said with a hint of annoyance in his voice. 'Besides, when would I have had the chance to do it?'

Greg stared at him. Sam had a point, now he thought about it. There hadn't really been an opportunity for Sam to sneak off up there to the bedroom. It didn't make any sense.

Sam climbed down off the stepladder. 'Show me,' he said.

Greg led the way upstairs. The hairs were prickling on the back of his neck and his palms felt sweaty. He had a sense of something being not quite right.

As they entered the bedroom, Sam walked across the floor and stood over the open board, staring down at it. He was suddenly silent.

Greg heard a soft *swish* and looked around. The bedroom door had closed. There was the quiet click of the lock.

Sam turned to look at him, and the expression on his face was both angry and frightened. 'I told you there was something weird about this game!' he said, his voice a low growl. 'Look at what's happened!'

Greg walked over to the board. He could see straight away that it had changed.

'That's not possible,' he breathed, staring at the board in disbelief. A feeling of panic churned in his stomach.

The coloured path still wound across the map – but now, most of the woodland that lay between the house and the town was gone, replaced by new buildings. And the town was different – there were more streets and more houses. And some of the old houses had been replaced by new ones.

Greg stared at their school. That hadn't been there before.

And the multistorey car park had appeared as well.

So had the shopping centre.

The map on the board still covered the same area – but somehow it had been *updated*.

Greg looked up at Sam. 'How did this happen?' he breathed.

Sam didn't reply.

And then Greg noticed something else that almost stopped his heart. The two figures that stood on the board had been repainted – the one on the ladder square had brown hair and was wearing a red top and black trousers. The other one had blond hair and was dressed in a white top and blue trousers.

Greg stared up at his blond-haired friend, in his white shirt and blue jeans. He looked down at his own clothes.

Red T-shirt and black trousers.

He fought desperately against the madness of it – he *knew* things like this couldn't happen. It had to be a trick of some sort. A joke.

'No!' Greg gasped. 'It's not real! It can't be real!'

'I'm going,' Sam said, his voice thick in his throat. He turned, but as he did so, his shoe caught the cup which was standing unnoticed at his feet. The cup rolled over and the dice spilled out.

They came up five.

Greg gave a hiss of fear as he saw Sam's piece quiver and shudder. Entirely unaided, it moved five squares forward on the board.

Greg scrambled away across the carpet and Sam ran for the door. He grabbed the handle and twisted it, but the door remained closed. He struggled with the handle for a few moments then turned, his back to the door, staring across the room at the game, panting and wide-eyed.

'It's alive!' Sam shouted. 'You have to make it stop!'

'I'll smash it up,' Greg gasped. Slowly, reluctantly, he crawled across the carpet towards the board game. Up till then he had wanted to believe that someone was playing tricks on them – but there was no way of explaining away the fact that he had seen Sam's piece move on its own.

'Quickly!' Sam shouted, his voice filled with panic, still tugging at the door handle. 'Before it does something else to us!'

Greg reached out and tried to flip the board

closed. But it was as though it was glued to the carpet. He stretched his fingers towards his piece. Swallowing his fear, he closed his fist around it. A moment later he fell back with a yell. It had been hot – too hot to touch. It had burned his hand.

While he was still recovering from the burning pain, he saw the rule book quivering on the carpet. The pages began to turn as though the booklet was caught in a fierce wind.

The fluttering of the pages stopped and Greg felt a strange, horrible compulsion to crawl over to it and to see what the open pages showed.

In pale, faded handwriting he saw:

Vital Rules for Good Luck, Bad Luck.
1. *Players MUST take their turn in the right order.*
2. *Players MUST finish the game.*

He looked around at Sam. 'We have to finish the game,' he said, his voice a strained croak. 'It says so . . . in the rules.'

Sam shook his head. Greg could see that his friend was terrified. Sam turned and struggled with the door handle again. The door didn't open. He thumped on the door with both fists. 'Get me out of here!' he screamed at the closed door in frustration.

From downstairs, Greg could hear music on the radio in the kitchen. Edie had her pop music at full volume, and it was playing loud enough to blot out any noise they might make.

'Don't you get it?' Greg shouted at Sam. 'It won't let us out till we finish the game!'

'Mrs Crowley!' Sam shouted, still beating at the door. 'Help! Mrs Crowley!'

Greg scrambled to his feet and ran over to his friend. He grabbed him by the shoulder. 'It's pointless!' he said. 'We have to finish the game.'

'I'm not going near that thing,' Sam said. Greg had never seen his friend like this.

'It's the only way,' Greg said. 'Listen to me!' He punched Sam's arm to get his attention. Sam stared at him, wild-eyed and panting. 'Maybe we don't need to play the entire game,' Greg said. 'Maybe if one of us lands on a good-luck square we'll find a way to escape.'

As he turned towards the game, a sudden thought struck him.

What kind of square had Sam's piece landed on after that last move?

Good luck or bad luck?

A brown bird was drawn on Sam's square.

Greg sat back on his heels, puzzled. *A brown bird.* Was that good luck or bad luck? He stared at the rule book, lying open on the carpet. He picked it up and went through it. Amazingly, there didn't seem to be any explanation of what the symbols meant.

Sam was still standing by the door, quiet now but still looking frightened.

'I can't figure it out,' Greg said. 'A bird could mean anything. I know magpies are one for sorrow, and two for joy . . . but magpies are black and white and the bird here is brown – like a sparrow or something.'

He looked at Sam. 'Do you know any superstitions that involve sparrows?'

Sam shook his head.

'No,' Greg said. 'Me neither.' He took a long, deep breath. 'Oh, well – only one thing for it,' he said. He picked up the cup and dropped the dice into it.

'Don't,' Sam said.

Greg looked at him. 'Chill out – I'm feeling lucky,' he said. It wasn't true, but he couldn't think of what else to say. They had to find a way of getting out of that room – they *had* to beat the game somehow. There would be plenty of time to go crazy thinking about exactly what was going on here afterwards. He hoped.

He shook the cup and rolled the dice.

'Seven,' he said. His heart thundered as he waited for his piece to move itself. But nothing happened. He let out a breath. 'Well, at least that's an improvement,' he said. He reached out cautiously. The piece was cool to his trembling fingertips. He paced out seven squares. He looked around at Sam. 'It's one of those yellow squares.'

'You need to take a card, then,' Sam said. He seemed to have calmed down a bit, and walked slowly across the floor and stood beside Greg.

Greg lifted the top card off the deck and turned it over.

In that same faded handwriting he read the words:

Survival Card: What's the Worst That Can Happen?
Better Keep Your Fingers Crossed!

'That's not so bad,' Greg said. 'What do you think it means?'

'I'm guessing it means cross your fingers and hope for the best,' Sam said, squatting beside Greg and holding both his hands up. His fingers were already tightly crossed.

'Good idea,' Greg said, crossing his own fingers. 'It's your turn.'

'I know,' Sam said. He squatted there, staring at the board for several long, silent seconds.

'Well?' said Greg.

'OK, I'm just . . . you know . . .' Sam had a bit of trouble getting the dice back into the cup without uncrossing his fingers, but he managed it in the end. Then he picked up the cup between his two hands and shook it.

The dice spilled out.

Both of them landed six up.

'Twelve,' Greg said. 'That's got to be good luck.'

Sam pushed his piece along the board with the edge of his hand.

Greg peered at the square. It was dark blue, with a bright yellow zigzag line running across it.

'I'm not sure what that's meant to be,' he said. 'You look.'

Sam leaned forward. His voice was low. 'I think it's a streak of lightning,' he said. He looked at Greg and there was fear in his eyes. 'Does that mean I'm going to be struck by lightning?' he breathed anxiously.

Greg looked out of the window. 'Not today. There isn't a cloud in the sky. And it probably won't happen at all if you do what the card says and keep your fingers crossed.'

'That was *your* card,' Sam said. 'What makes you think it's going to help me?'

Before Greg got the chance to reply, his attention was taken by a curious fluttering noise. He looked around, trying to pinpoint the direction from which it was coming.

Sam was staring at the old fireplace. The hearth was empty except for an ornamental poker and a polished brass coal scuttle. The fluttering sound became more frantic – it reminded Greg of the noise a flag makes when it's caught in a strong wind.

Sam stood up and moved towards the fireplace. 'There's something—'

He got no further. A ragged shape suddenly burst out of the fireplace – flying into Sam's face and then veering away at the last moment in a flurry of sooty wings.

Sam reeled back, his hands up to cover his face.

Greg clambered to his feet, watching the small shape as it circled the room. It was a sparrow. Somehow, it must have fallen into the chimney.

The bird made for the light of the windows. It got tangled for a moment in the net curtains, then managed to free itself and continued its wild circling of the room. It was in a total panic.

Greg ran over to the window, threw the net curtain aside and tried to lift the sash, but it wouldn't budge. Seeing the bright light over his shoulder, the sparrow came careering towards the window. It crashed into the glass with a wild flapping of wings and then was gone again – darting around the room in blind terror.

Greg saw Sam run at the bird with a look of pure fear in his eyes.

'I'll get you!' he shouted. Greg saw with horror that Sam was holding the poker from the fireplace, swinging it wildly at the bird.

'Sam! Stop!' Greg called.

'It's going to give me bad luck!' Sam shouted.

'Sam – you're crazy!' Greg called out. 'Leave it alone – it can't hurt you!'

'No! I've got to stop it!' Sam shouted. 'Otherwise something bad will happen!'

'It's just a harmless bird!' Greg screamed at his friend.

'The game sent it!' Sam screamed, swinging the poker wildly. 'I have to kill it!'

Exhausted, the bird came to rest for a moment on an old-fashioned brass wall light beside the bed.

'No!' Greg shouted.

But Sam wasn't listening. He was only a couple of metres away from the bird now. Greg could see its little chest rising and falling – its tiny eyes wide and alert.

Sam raised the poker above his head.

'Sam – be careful!' Greg shouted. 'Watch out for the light!'

'I'll get you!' Sam yelled, lunging forwards. He brought the poker down with a cry.

The sparrow was gone from the light fitting in a flash. But Sam couldn't stop the momentum of his blow. The poker crashed against the light fitting. One brass arm broke away and fell to the floor.

There was a dreadful hissing and spitting sound. Smoke poured from the light fitting, and there were white and blue sparks. Greg suddenly realized what was happening.

His friend was being electrocuted.

Smoke rose from the poker and there was a horrible smell of burning. Sam's hair was on end and his mouth was wide open – his lips drawn back in a silent scream.

Greg sprang forwards, crashing into Sam and dragging him off his feet.

The poker came away from the wall. There was a loud bang and a ball of thick black smoke gushed out of the light fitting.

Sam and Greg fell together on to the carpet. Sam's body was rigid – and he was still clutching the poker.

'*Sam*, are you all right?' Greg gasped, almost

choking with horror and nausea.

'Sam?' He shook his friend's shoulders. *'Sam!'* But there was no response.

The smell of burning skin was making Greg retch. Fighting for breath, he pulled himself away from Sam, who was lying on his side. His hands were horribly blackened and still smouldering. He seemed to be unconscious.

Suddenly, the bedroom door burst open. Greg's mother appeared in the doorway.

'All the electrics have gone out,' she shouted. 'What on earth's happened?'

Greg stared at her. 'Call an ambulance,' he gasped, tears running down his face. 'Sam's been hurt. It was the game! The game did it!'

Greg and his mother were sitting in the waiting area outside the hospital ward. It was the evening, and they were waiting for the nurse to say they could go in and see Sam. It felt to Greg like they'd been waiting for days.

Greg's mother looked closely into his eyes.

'Are you feeling better now?' she asked.

Greg nodded.

She stroked his hair. 'You had me worried for a while there,' she said with a faint smile. 'All that strange stuff you were saying about the game.'

Greg gazed at her. He was shattered. All he wanted to do right then was to find a little hole somewhere, climb into it and close it up behind him.

The memory of what had happened in the aftermath of Sam's accident was fuzzy in his brain. He knew he had been babbling about the game. He had told his mother that it was alive and out to get them. He had told her how the game wouldn't let them stop playing – how the board couldn't be moved.

After the paramedics had come and Sam had been taken away to hospital, his mum had folded the board up without any trouble. Greg had noticed that the board no longer had the updated town on it – it had gone back to the way it had looked when they had first found it. His mother had put the pieces and the cards and the booklet back into the box and shut the lid. The two figures were back to normal. And the door must have unlocked itself.

A nurse approached Greg and his mother.

'You can go and see him now,' she said. 'He's still a little groggy, so you won't get much out of him.'

'We just want to let him know we're thinking of him,' said Greg's mother.

Sam was in a small side ward. There were only four beds and his was the only one occupied. Greg was startled by how small his friend looked in the hospital bed. Sam lay there, his face ashen and his arms resting on the covers. Both of his hands were heavily bandaged.

'Hello, Sam,' Mrs Crowley said gently, leaning over the bed. 'How are you doing?'

He blinked up at her. 'OK,' he whispered.

'That's good,' said Mrs Crowley. 'Tell you what – I'll leave you two alone to chat for a few minutes.'

She smiled down at him. 'I'm glad you're feeling better, Sam.'

'Thanks.'

'I'll be just outside, when you're ready,' Mrs Crowley said to Greg.

He nodded, watching her as she left the room. When he turned back to Sam, he saw fear in his friend's eyes.

'We didn't get to finish the game,' Sam said.

'Yes, we did,' Greg said gently. 'Mum put it away.'

Sam looked at him. 'Is it going to stay put away, though?' he asked.

'It's just an old game,' Greg said fiercely. 'A stupid, old-fashioned, ordinary board game.'

'Is that what you *really* believe?' Sam asked.

Greg gnawed his lower lip, avoiding Sam's eyes. 'I don't know.' If he refused to admit it out loud, maybe he could convince himself that the game wasn't really alive after all – that it wasn't really so terrible.

Sam raised his arms. 'Look at what it did to me,' he said. 'You can't pretend it never happened.'

Greg winced as he looked at his friend's bandaged hands. 'I know,' he said. He gave Sam a desperate look. 'But maybe it's finished with us now.'

'It should be smashed up or burned or something,' Sam said quietly.

Greg looked at him. 'I'm not going near it again,' he said quietly. 'Not ever.'

Sam closed his eyes, saying nothing.

Greg stood there for a few moments, unable to think of a single thing to say to his injured friend.

The silence became uncomfortable.

'I think I'll go home now,' Greg said at last.

'Fine,' Sam said.

Greg looked anxiously at his friend. 'I can't go back there,' he said. 'I can't.'

Sam didn't respond.

'I'm really sorry you got hurt,' Greg blurted. He walked quickly to the door and pushed through it. He looked back at his friend as the door began to close.

A dart of anguish pierced his heart. Sam was

sitting bolt upright in the bed. He was staring around the room as if he was still searching for the trapped bird – and there was a haunted, frightened look in his eyes.

'I know you've had enough for one day,' Mrs Crowley said as they climbed into the car, 'but I promised Mr Shepherd at the nursing home that I'd pop in for a quick word with him this evening. Apparently your gran's been a bit unsettled the last couple of days.' She glanced at him. 'You don't mind, do you? It'll only take a few minutes.'

'I don't mind,' Greg said vaguely. He was still thinking about the expression he had seen on Sam's face as they had left him. It had been very scary – and somehow *familiar*. And then it struck him. It was the same bewildered, distressed look that he had often seen on his gran's face.

While his mother had her quick word with Mr Shepherd, Greg found himself drawn to his gran's room. If she was having a good day, he was going to ask her about that game. He had some very serious questions he needed answers to.

He knocked and opened the door to her room. The TV was on – some game show or other. Gran was sitting up in a nest of pillows, staring vacantly at the screen, her gnarled old arthritic hands resting on the bedcovers.

She turned her head at the sound of him coming into the room, her bleary eyes narrowing.

'Hi, Gran. It's me, Greg.'

She grimaced and made an incoherent noise in her throat.

'Gran – it's OK. It's Greg.'

She shifted uneasily in the bed, trying to focus on him.

'Get away!' she moaned. 'You never give me any peace. Get away from me!'

She brought her arms up as if to protect her face. Her crippled hands flailed.

Greg took a step towards the bed and then froze.

He had never noticed before – he always avoided

looking too closely at her twisted hands. But he noticed now.

His gran's fingers were crossed.

'Leave me be!' his gran groaned. 'For pity's sake – after all these years, can't you just leave me be!'

Greg moved towards the bed. 'Gran! It's me!'

'No! No! No!'

Greg caught her thrashing arms. 'Gran! Stop it. I need to talk to you about the Good Luck, Bad Luck game. We found it in your wardrobe at the house.'

Her eyes widened in terror and she began to scream.

'Gran! Please!'

But the old lady was wild with fear. Greg backed away from her. He had no idea how to cope with her in that state.

A nurse came running into the room. 'What did you do?' she asked.

'Nothing,' Greg gasped. 'Nothing.'

'Now, now, Lizzie, what's all this noise for?' The nurse reached for a buzzer on a cord that hung at the head of the bed. She looked at Greg. 'I'll need help with her. Don't worry, we'll get her settled – but it's probably best if you leave her with me.'

Confused, Greg backed out of the room. He closed his eyes and leaned against the wall out in the corridor, taking long, heaving breaths like someone bursting up into the air out of deep, dark water. He was trembling all over – his legs felt so weak that he could hardly stand.

He was vaguely aware of people going into his gran's room. The shrill screaming died away and a strange silence replaced it.

He opened his eyes, suddenly filled with a new determination. No matter how scary it would be, he knew what he had to do.

He ran along the corridor, passing the office where his mother was speaking with Mr Shepherd. He ran down the stairs, across the reception area and out through the front double doors.

Something had just fallen into place in his head. Neither he nor Sam had been able to work out where the game had ended on the old version of the board. It had been somewhere in town. And when the board had updated itself, they had been so shocked that neither of them had thought to check it out. But now Greg knew exactly where that winding path of coloured squares came to an end.

It ended at the nursing home. *The nursing home that had once been a lunatic asylum.*

He ran along the street, ignoring the curious glances of the people he sped past. He didn't hear the horns of the cars blaring as he ran heedlessly in front of them. He had only one idea burning in his mind: to get to his grandparents' house and destroy that game!

He ran across town and into the park. A stitch was biting into his side, but he ran on. Now he could see the chimney tops of the house in amongst the trees.

He came to the wrought-iron gate and walked up the path. The front door was open a fraction. He assumed that the latch hadn't caught properly when they had left the house earlier.

Inside, the house was eerily quiet. As if it was holding its breath. Waiting for something.

Waiting for him?

He stood at the foot of the stairs. Gripping the banister rail, he could feel the hairs prickle on the back of his neck.

Slowly and determinedly, he mounted the stairs.

From the top, he could see that the bedroom door was closed. The walls and the floor seemed to reel and shift around him. The blood sang in his ears. Walking slowly along the landing, he reached forward, turned the door handle and pushed it open. He could feel his stomach turn – there was still a smell of scorching.

For a moment or two he didn't dare to look at that place on the carpet where the board had been set up.

What if it was there again?

He took a deep breath and turned his head.

He gasped.

The carpet was bare.

Still trembling a little, he walked over to the wardrobe. He was going to rip that board to pieces – then he was going to smash the box and tear up the cards and the booklet. Then he'd break those two figures into small splinters.

And then the game wouldn't be able to hurt anyone ever again.

But the game wasn't in there.

He heard giggling coming from nearby.

He spun around – it was Edie's voice.

She must have come back here on her own.

'Edie?' he called, running to the door. *'Edie?'*

The door to one of the rooms along the landing was slightly ajar. As he approached, he heard Edie's voice coming from inside the room.

'I found it!' she called. 'I *knew* the two of you were doing something in there yesterday when you wouldn't let me in. You tried to hide it from me – but I came back and I found it!'

'Edie – what are you doing here?' Greg shouted. 'What are you talking about?'

'I want us to play the game!' Edie shouted.

Greg's stopped dead still. His whole body felt cold. He pushed the door wide open, already knowing what he would see, hoping desperately that he was wrong.

Edie was sitting cross-legged on the floor. The board game was set up in front of her. There were two figures standing on the board.

Edie had her fingers tightly crossed in her lap.

Greg stepped into the room and the door swung closed. 'Edie, no . . .' he breathed.

'I've had my first go,' Edie said, grinning up at him. 'It's your turn now.'

GHOST IN THE MACHINE

'You're going to crash!' Rory McBride shouted to his sister. 'Slow down or you won't make the bend!'

'Will you shut up! I know what I'm doing!' April yelled back.

The car took the curve at high speed, and for a few moments it really did look to Rory as if April might make it – but then the back wheels began to skid uncontrollably. A split second later, the front wheels hit the kerb and there was a kaleidoscope of movement through the windscreen as the car left the road and tumbled over and over through the air. The scream of torn and smashed metal ended with a sickening thud as the car hit a wall and exploded.

There was a white flare, and red letters jumped on to the screen.

You Are So Dead! Game Over, Rookie!

'Rats!' April spat, dropping the control console into her lap. 'I was going too fast.'

'*Told* you so,' said Rory with a grin. He was thirteen, a year older than his sister, and they both shared a passion for driving simulation games.

'Shift over,' he said. 'It's my turn.'

April tossed her long black hair and narrowed her eyes in annoyance. Rory knew how badly she wanted to beat him. *In her dreams!* he thought to himself.

'You think you drive better than me?' she said,

raising an eyebrow. 'I don't think so! You're just lucky.'

'I'm a *totally* better driver than you,' Rory said.

April's eyes glittered with the challenge. 'If you say that boys make better drivers than girls, I'll kick you in the head till you see stars, OK?'

'Can't take the truth, eh?' laughed Rory, hitting the 'reload' button on the console.

'Well – for a start, Mum's a better driver than Dad,' April said, poking him in the ribs with her toes.

'No way!' Rory replied, trying to fend off her attack.

'She *so* is,' said April.

There was the sound of a car drawing up in front of the house. April jumped up and ran to the window. 'That'll be her now – I'll go and ask her who's the better driver.'

'Oh, right! Like Mum would admit that Dad's better,' Rory replied.

'Oh, no!' gasped April, staring out of the lounge window. 'We'd better get outside, Rory.'

'What's up?' Rory asked, his eyes still on the TV screen. But April left the room without replying.

Puzzled, Rory got up and stared out of the window. It was Mum in the family car, but there was clearly something wrong. Black smoke was billowing out from under the bonnet. His mum was standing there, her hands planted on her hips.

Rory ran into the hallway and out through the front door. April was already on the pavement, standing next to Mum.

'What's happened?' he said, as a plume of black smoke rose slowly up over the car.

'Don't ask me,' his mother replied. 'It started doing this when I was in town. I only just managed to get it back here.'

Rory heard feet on the stairs behind him. A moment later, his father was standing at his side, staring at the smoking car. 'Elaine, what have you done?' he asked.

Oh no, thought Rory. *That was definitely the wrong thing to say*.

'Excuse me?' Rory's mum said in a frosty tone.

'You've done it now, Dad,' Rory whispered to his dad as his mum marched over towards them.

'What have *I* done, Michael? I'll tell you what *I've* done – I've made an executive decision about this horrible old wreck of a car. We're getting a new one, OK? One that's reliable, comfortable and easy to run. And this is *not* up for discussion.'

Rory's mum had the same fierce grey eyes as April. When she unleashed one of the looks that Rory referred to as her 'death stare', no one argued back.

'I'm not sure we can afford a new car right now,' Mr McBride began tentatively. 'It might not be anything particularly serious. I'll take it to the garage tomorrow afternoon, and—'

Rory's mother pointed at the car. 'I hate this machine,' she said. 'And it hates me. We hate each other! We are getting a new car, Michael.'

'There's a huge new showroom on the other side of town,' April added. 'I saw something about it in the local paper. The advert said they have some great opening deals – and they take part-exchange.'

Rory quickly chose to side with his mum – he really liked the idea of them getting a new, cooler car. 'Come on, Dad! It'll be brilliant. We could go and look round the showroom tomorrow – I'll help you choose!'

'Hey, me too!' April added. 'You can't rely on Rory, Dad – he'll just pick something flashy and fast. You're going to need sensible advice on all the fittings, like a good stereo and a satellite navigation system and stuff like that.'

'That's decided, then,' said Mrs McBride, giving one last disdainful look at the smoking car. 'The two of you can go with your father to the showroom. I'm going to be stuck in the office tomorrow – there's a big all-day meeting with some clients from abroad – so I'm going to have to trust the three of you to pick the perfect car without me. Think *luxury*, Michael,' she said, winking. 'And listen to the kids!'

'Don't worry, Mum,' Rory said. 'We'll make sure Dad buys something good.'

'Admit it, Dad. You're lost, aren't you?' Rory asked, looking at his dad from the passenger seat. They'd finally got the car working again, though Rory reckoned that it was on its last legs.

'I'm *not* lost,' his father replied. 'I'm taking the scenic route, that's all.'

Rory stared out at the grey warehouses that lined the street and sighed. 'Dad, you are the *worst* navigator in the whole world. We should have gone back for the street map like I said right at the start.'

'I know where we're going, Rory,' said his father testily. 'It was that stupid diversion that put me off. How was I supposed to know they had suddenly decided to dig up the main street across town?'

'Which is exactly why you need a good navigation system in the new car,' April piped up. 'That way, you can just tell it where you want to go, and it'll let you know the best way of getting there.'

'Or I could remember to bring the street map,' her father muttered, craning his neck to see what the hold-up was.

'That didn't help you find the way to our holiday cottage last summer,' April reminded him. 'Mum said that you were driving in the wrong direction, but you didn't believe her *or* the road map!'

'And you got lost trying to find that big new shopping centre out of town, remember?' Rory added with a grin. 'And what about that time . . .'

'I get the picture,' his father interrupted. 'Your daft dad can't find his way out of a paper bag. OK, I surrender – we'll get a satellite navigation system. Happy?'

'We could use a sat-nav right now,' April mumbled. 'We are *never* going to find the showroom.'

Her father turned the car along another street. 'Aha!' he said brightly. 'I recognize this. Yes.' He gave a whoop of delight. 'I know *exactly* where we are. The showroom is about five minutes away.' The car sped up. 'Satellite navigation!' their dad snorted. 'Who needs it?'

* * *

Rory thought the car showroom was really impressive. It was located in a new industrial estate – a long, low ultra-modern building that stretched out behind a broad forecourt. It had a massive stretch of reflective glass along the front, and long banners and trailing pennants displaying special opening offers and bargains.

A dozen or more shiny new cars stood out on the forecourt under fluttering gold and silver bunting. More expensive models were displayed on raised plinths inside.

Mr McBride parked their car and they got out. Rory saw several smartly dressed salespeople looking at them as they walked on to the forecourt.

'Hello, there – may I help you?' asked one young man with an ultra-sharp haircut and a smile like a camera flashbulb.

'We're just looking at the moment,' replied Mr McBride.

Rory grinned – he could see that his dad wasn't

going to be rushed. But there were some amazing cars here – picking one was going to be tricky.

They wound their way through the display models. April wandered from car to car, and Rory peered in through the polished windows, drooling over the luxurious interiors and state-of-the-art technology.

'It's so hard to choose,' April said, standing by a car with flame-red paintwork. 'Can we have two, Dad?'

'Four would be better,' Rory called after his father, who had moved on. 'That's one each!'

'Just as soon as I win the lottery!' their father called back.

Rory spotted April hovering in front of a particular car. 'Hey, Dad!' she yelled. 'I've found one that Mum will go totally crazy about! Come and look.'

Rory and his dad approached the car.

A sales lady came over to help. 'It has all the features the discerning driver needs,' she said. 'ABS, on-board computer, cruise control, front and rear air bags. It also has a multi-disc CD boot-changer and driver and passenger climate controls.'

'Does it have sat-nav?' April asked.

'That's an optional extra,' the sales lady said. 'We have several different versions and we have trained mechanics on stand-by who can fit the system of your choice within the hour.'

Mr McBride pursed his lips, staring at the price sticker on the windscreen.

'Well—' he began, but Rory interrupted.

'We can afford it, can't we, Dad?' Rory said.

'Think how happy it would make Mum, not only to have a great car but for us not to get lost any more!' April added.

'We can arrange very generous financing terms, sir,' the sales lady added quickly. 'The paperwork won't take more than ten minutes.' She smiled at April and Rory. 'You could drive it away this afternoon! But I don't want to rush you . . . feel free to have a good look around. You won't find any better deals, I can promise you that.'

'So?' April said. 'Are we going to buy this wonderful, beautiful, fabulous car – or do you want to look at some others first, Dad?'

Her father looked at the car. 'Do you think Mum will like it?' he asked.

'She'll love it!' Rory said. 'It's awesome, Dad.'

Mr McBride walked around the car. 'Let's take it for a drive, then,' he said.

'And then can we buy it?' April said.

'We'll see,' said her father.

'It'll drive like a dream,' April said, smiling. 'I just know it!'

Rory really enjoyed the test drive. April had been right: the car moved like a total dream, and the luxurious interior smelled of new leather and polish.

The sales lady got out of the front passenger seat and held the back door open for Rory and April to scramble out. She smiled at Mr McBride over the car's shiny roof. 'What did you think?' she asked.

'It's not a bad car,' Mr McBride replied, stroking

his chin thoughtfully. 'No, not bad at all.'

'Come off it, Dad!' said Rory. 'You know you *totally* love it!'

Their father looked at Rory and April and nodded. 'OK,' he said, smiling at the sales lady. 'We'll take it!'

'And don't forget to get a navigation system,' Rory reminded him.

'A really good one,' April added.

'OK, kids,' he said. 'It's going to take them a little while to fit the navigation system – how about we go and find somewhere for a bite to eat while we're waiting?'

'You made sure we got the best sat-nav, didn't you, Dad?' April asked. 'One of those brilliant ones that get their instructions straight from the satellite?'

'I didn't think we needed anything too complicated,' said their father. 'The one I bought was half the price of the top-end versions,' he said. 'But it has all the features we need. And the lady told me that there's a website where you can download new information as regularly as you need to. Apparently, the updated information can be loaded straight into the unit from a PC!'

April frowned at him. 'The modern ones do that stuff automatically,' she said.

'Yes, and they cost twice the amount of the one I got,' their father replied. 'It'll be great, you'll see. And by the way – as it was you two who insisted we needed the thing in the first place – I'm relying on you to figure out how to use it!'

'Well – this is great,' said Mr McBride. 'So much for your new technology!'

Rory peered out at the 'Road Closed' sign directly ahead of them. Things had been going fine up until then. Rory had read the manual and had programmed in their home address. At first, his dad seemed to be enjoying the new gadget – grinning every time the woman's pleasant mechanical voice gave them new instructions.

But his smile and cheery mood faded very quickly

when they hit the roadworks that had closed the main bridge over the river.

'So, how come the sat-nav didn't know about all this?' Mr McBride asked. 'Isn't that exactly the kind of thing it ought to warn us about? I'd be better off listening to the local radio station – at least they keep up to date.' He poked at the controls on the dashboard.

'Don't panic, Dad,' Rory said, pushing his father's hand aside and quickly finding the local news channel. 'It'll work brilliantly once we've downloaded the Web updates.'

'It better had,' grumbled his father, putting the car in reverse and manoeuvring it on to the road that led alongside the river.

As they drove along, Rory looked back over his shoulder. He could see that the entire middle section of the bridge was missing. These were major roadworks and then some! Their only choice now was to go right around to the other bridge – a much longer route home. And to make matters worse, black clouds were gathering and it was just beginning to rain.

'Marvellous!' groaned their dad. 'Now the rain is going to ruin the wax finish before your mum even gets a chance to see it!'

'Look on the bright side,' Rory said, pointing to the swishing windscreen wipers. 'The rain sensor meant that they came on automatically.'

'Hmm – well, I suppose that is something,' his father said, leaning forwards and pressing the 'off' button on the sat-nav.

'*Goodbye,*' the robotic female voice said.

'And goodbye to you, too!' replied their father.

A jagged fork of lightning lit the sky for a moment.

'One . . . two . . . three . . . four . . .' Rory counted. A peal of thunder followed it. 'That means the storm is about two kilometres away,' he said in his best scientist voice.

'It'll pass,' his father said, having to speak loudly as the hammering of rain on the roof threatened to drown him out. 'You'll see.'

As they drove along, a second fork of lightning split the sky open for a second.

'One . . . two . . .' Thunder rumbled. 'It's getting closer,' Rory said. 'It'll be right on top of us soon. And it sounds like it's going to be a really bad one!'

'So? Do you like it?' Mr McBride asked his wife. Rory, April and their mum and dad were standing in the shelter of the front porch. The new car was parked in the drive for Mrs McBride to look at.

'Like it?' said their mother. 'I think so, but I can hardly see it!'

Rory gave a rueful smile. His mum was only exaggerating a little – the rain was now so heavy that the new car was behind a veil of falling water that bounced high off the roof and bonnet and ran in rivers down the grey tarmac of the drive.

She looked at April and Rory. 'What do you both think?' she asked.

'We love it,' Rory said.

'We could go for a ride in the rain,' said their father. 'Elaine? What about it?'

Their mother stared up at the heaving black clouds. 'Oh, why not?' she said with a smile. 'I'm driving. You kids coming?'

'We've got the sat-nav to update!' Rory replied.

'He'll need my help, since I'm a better driver than Rory,' April grinned, pushing her brother in the back.

'Go and get what you need from the car, and then we'll be off,' their dad said.

Rory ran through the heavy rain, his T-shirt instantly sticking to his back. He took the sat-nav from its perch on the dashboard and grabbed the manual and PC connector lead from the glove compartment.

'Got it!' he shouted, running back towards the house, cradling everything under the front of his T-shirt to keep it dry. As soon as he got back into the doorway, April snatched the sat-nav and its accessories.

'I'll take those!' she said.

Mr McBride lifted his coat up over his wife's head. 'Ready? Set? Go!' he called, and Rory and April watched as their parents raced out into the pelting rain.

A huge jagged fork of lightning lit up the sky and thunder boomed directly overhead. On the whole, Rory liked thunderstorms – but this one felt a bit too close for comfort.

Rory waved, but his mum and dad didn't seem to notice. 'Be careful!' he said, more to himself than anyone else. He watched the rain bouncing and bubbling on the path for a few more moments.

'I'm going in,' April said. 'It's freezing out here!'

'See you in a minute,' replied Rory. He listened to the beating of the rain on the porch roof and the swirl of water in the gutters and drainpipes. It was a good job their house was on a hill – the way the rain was falling, some of the streets down by the river might actually get flooded. Rory stepped into the house and shut the door on the storm.

April was already in the computer room, seated at their PC, typing away. The monitor showed a colourful web page, on to which April was entering information about the family.

'You found the website OK, then?' Rory said.

'Easily,' April said. He could see that she had plugged the lead into the back of the navigation device and into a port on the PC.

'Do you want me to do the download for you?' Rory asked.

April looked at him. 'Hardly!'

'Is it all plugged in right?'

'Of *course* it is.' April flapped a hand at him. 'Don't breathe down my neck.'

'Don't mess it up.' Rory grinned.

'I *won't.*'

Rory watched as his sister located the web page that allowed customers to download updated information. She clicked on the 'download' tab and leaned back triumphantly, her arms folded. 'There – sorted!'

'Mum and Dad aren't going to have much fun, driving in this rain,' Rory said, looking out of the window. 'I bet they don't go far. If it doesn't let up soon, we'll—' But the rest of what he had intended to say was lost as the sky suddenly exploded into a blinding blaze of white light, accompanied by a blast of thunder that seemed to beat the house like a drum.

There was an explosion, like the firing of a shotgun right above their heads – a terrifying, deafening sound that made Rory throw his hands over his ears and duck down. The loud bang filled the air, accompanied by another flare of blue-white light. April let out a scream as the light bulbs overhead exploded.

Rory spun around and stared at the PC. Blue sparks were pouring from the monitor, and there was a crackling, fizzing noise.

'April – get away from there!' Rory pulled his sister away from the computer table.

'What happened?' April yelled.

A tongue of flame licked over the blackened plastic casing, then they were plunged into absolute darkness. Rory could feel April clinging to him, her fingers digging into his arms. He could hear her harsh, panicky breath over the pounding of the blood in his temples.

'Rory – what was that?' she gasped.

'I reckon the house was struck by lightning,' Rory breathed. 'Are you OK?'

'I think so. The computer blew up right in my face.'

'Are you hurt?'

'No. I'm fine. What happened to the lights?'

'I think the lightning must have wrecked all the electrics,' Rory said. 'Wow!' He looked at his sister and managed to raise a grin. 'We're lucky we weren't fried.' He clambered to his feet and looked out of the window. The streetlights were still on outside – and other houses glowed with light through the rain. 'It seems to have been just our house that got hit,' he said. 'I've got a torch in my room. Stay here, and I'll go and get it.'

'I'm coming with you,' April said as she got shakily to her feet. 'I'm not staying here on my own – the PC might burst into flames or something.'

'I suppose we should get the fire extinguisher from the cellar,' Rory said. 'Just to be on the safe side.' He carefully felt his way towards the door, circling the room to avoid going too close to the computer table. There was a nasty smell of melted plastic, and acrid smoke floated on the air.

They found a torch and made their way downstairs into the cellar. It was rather creepy to be down there without the lights on. Sinister black shadows loomed all around them in the torchlight, and the smell of burnt plastic was very strong.

Rory shone his torch on the main circuit box at the far end. 'April – look at this,' he breathed, his voice shaking. The box was melted. Wisps of grey smoke were filtering up from it. He peered at the blackened and misshapen box. 'It's a total mess,' he said.

'Do you think it's safe?' April asked. 'Might it catch fire?'

'I don't know.' Rory was reluctant to get any closer. 'Let's just grab the fire extinguisher and get out of here.' He looked at her. 'We ought to check around the house a bit – if the computer blew up, then other electric stuff might have done the same.'

They headed back to the stairs. Rory unclipped the small red fire extinguisher from the wall.

Rory led them in a quick check of all the downstairs rooms. Everything was in darkness, but there was no tell-tale smell of burnt plastic. It was beginning to look like the computer had taken the full force of the lightning strike.

They went back up to the computer room. Rory shone the torchlight on the computer. The monitor's flatscreen LCD panel had melted completely, and Rory could feel sticky pools of melted plastic crunching and squishing under his feet. One side of the computer was blackened and burnt away, but there was no sign that it might still be on fire.

'I think it's safe,' he said.

'It doesn't look too safe to me,' April said.

'I meant it doesn't look like it's going to catch fire,' Rory said. Then he remembered something which made the whole lightning strike even worse. 'The sat-nav! It was plugged in . . . it'll be a goner for sure,' he said.

'Oh *no*,' April groaned.

Rory traced the sat-nav lead from the back of the charred PC. Its other end was still plugged into the small navigation unit that was sitting on the edge of the table.

He shone the torch closer – hardly able to believe his eyes. The navigation device seemed untouched by the lightning strike. 'Hey – it looks OK,' he breathed.

April leaned close. 'That's amazing! Is it still working?'

Rory pressed the 'on' button. To his astonishment, the screen light came on, and the words 'download complete' appeared in large black letters.

'Awesome!' April breathed.

'It's completely OK,' Rory said. 'Unbelievable!'

'Let's get out of here,' April said. 'We'll get some help from next door till Mum and Dad get home.'

Rory nodded. They went downstairs, and he put the navigation unit on the hall stand. They had only gone a few steps when they saw the headlights of a car approaching.

'It's Mum and Dad!' Rory said in relief.

The car turned and glided into their driveway.

His mother's window slid down and she stared at him in surprise. 'What's going on?' she asked. 'Why are all the lights out?'

Rory helped his dad go around the house and unplug all the electrical items. Mr McBride gave a long, low whistle when he saw the damage to the computer. 'The strike must have gone straight for it,' he said, shaking his head. 'It's a definite insurance job. It's strange that nothing else appears to have been affected.' He shook his head. 'I don't know,' he added, looking at Rory. 'We leave you two alone for ten minutes and you manage to get the house struck by lightning.' He gave a lopsided, disbelieving smile. 'Typical.'

'It wasn't funny, Dad!' Rory said. 'We could have been blown to bits.'

'No,' his father said, his face suddenly serious again. 'I'm sure it wasn't in the least bit funny.' He reached out and patted Rory's shoulder. 'But look on the bright side: no one was hurt – and we're having an adventure in the dark.'

There was the sound of the front door opening and closing.

'That'll be April and your mum with dinner,' his father said. Sure enough, a few moments later, the two of them came into the room, accompanied by thick paper parcels and the smell of Chinese food.

After the meal, Mrs McBride took all the ice cream out of the freezer. 'No point in letting it defrost and go bad,' she smiled, handing out spoons.

She had made the house feel really cosy, lighting plenty of candles in the kitchen and the lounge and some more in carefully chosen places in the hallway and on the upper landing.

Maybe the power being out isn't such a bad thing, Rory thought as he scooped out another spoonful of chocolate chip ice cream. *Like Dad said – it's a bit of an adventure.*

Just then, something caught his eye. 'That's odd,' Rory said aloud. The green timer light on the microwave was flashing on and off. 'I'm *sure* it wasn't doing that before.' When he and his dad had checked the house, there had been no sign of anything electrical working.

The timer showed four zeros – slowly blinking on and off. It looked a little eerie in the candlelight. Mrs McBride went over to it and pressed some buttons – but the flashing row of zeros didn't change.

'It's definitely not working,' she said.

'I shouldn't imagine it is,' said Mr McBride. 'I unplugged it.'

'So why's the light still on?' Rory asked.

'Some sort of internal battery, I suppose,' said his

father. 'Lots of household devices have emergency batteries to keep the clocks running when the power goes.'

'So why is it just showing noughts?' April asked.

'Beats me,' her father said. 'Now then – who's for a game of Cluedo by candlelight?'

Everyone headed for the living-room. Rory was last out, and as he left, he glanced over his shoulder. He froze. For an instant the flashing display had looked different.

Instead of the four zeros, he could have sworn he saw the word *RO:RY*.

He blinked and looked again. This time the clock read four zeros again.

'Hey, come on, slowcoach!' April called from the living-room. 'There's a murder to be solved in here!'

Feeling a little unsettled, Rory headed for the lounge.

That night, Rory lay in bed with his hands folded behind his head, staring up into the darkness. He had never even considered before how many totally ordinary things he used every day were dependent on electricity.

With the power out, the family had been reduced to sitting on the living-room carpet playing Cluedo in a ring of tea lights. Once they'd finished the game, he couldn't even crash out in front of the TV or listen to his music. And candlelight might look nice, but he and April were *way* too old for the ghost stories that Dad was desperate to tell them.

He turned over in bed and pulled the covers over his ears. Hopefully the emergency electrician would be there first thing in the morning – and then they'd be able to get back to normal. But sleep felt a long way off. He lay tossing and turning, unable to get comfortable.

In the darkness behind his closed eyelids he could still see the microwave's green display panel.

00:00. *RO:RY*. 00:00.

He sat up, forcing his eyes open – forcing the image out of his head.

'It wasn't real!' he whispered aloud to himself. 'I imagined it.' He lay back, eyes wide, determined to force the disturbing image out of his head.

He let his eyes close.

The eerie green lights came floating back.

Eventually he drifted off into troubled sleep, but the flashing display was with him all night.

The electrician lifted his baseball cap and scratched at his closely shaven head. 'That must have been some lightning strike,' he said, illuminating the damaged fuse box with the light of a large, square torch. 'I've never seen anything like this before. The fuses are melted together.'

It was about ten o'clock the next morning. Mr McBride was with the electrician down in the cellar. Rory and April were perched on the steps, listening to what the man had to say.

'Can you fix it?' April asked.

'It'll take a while,' he said. 'But I'll get the power back on for you, don't worry.' He stared at the melted box. 'What I can't figure out is that the water pipes and the copper in the electrical circuitry should have earthed the strike. Nothing should have blown up. You should have been perfectly fine – I don't understand it. I'll just go and get my gear from the van and then I'll get to work.'

'Is it OK if I watch?' Rory asked.

'Don't be a nuisance, Rory,' said his father.

'That's not a problem,' said the electrician. 'I don't mind an audience. And he can hold the torch for me.'

Both April and Rory hung around to share duties in holding the powerful torch and fetching the electrician cold drinks and biscuits.

It was mid-morning before he had finally replaced and rewired the main fuse box.

'Switch the light on, Rory,' he said. Rory reached up and flicked the light switch for the cellar. Nothing happened.

'Uh-oh,' Rory said.

The electrician laughed. 'April – come here, will you? You can do the honours.'

April stood next to him.

'See the red lever?' he said. 'Pull it down for me.'

'I won't get blown up, will I?' she asked.

'No, I promise you won't get blown up,' the electrician said.

April flipped the lever on the side of the new fuse box.

All three of the bulbs in the cellar went on. 'And that's magic!' the electrician said.

'Will everything be OK now?' Rory asked.

'I don't see why not,' said the electrician, gathering his tools.

'The computer won't be,' said April glumly. 'It's totally wrecked.'

After the electrician had left, April and Rory ran into the lounge and put on their favourite music channel on TV.

'That's the last of the peace and quiet, I suppose,' said Dad, sitting down with his newspaper.

'So when will we get the new computer, Dad?' April asked.

'Can we help choose it?' Rory added. 'There's this great flatscreen one that my friend Matt's got—'

'Stop right there, Rory,' his dad said. 'That won't be an issue till we get the insurance money. I've phoned them and set the wheels in motion, but I'm afraid you might have to do without a computer for a few weeks.'

Rory and April looked at one another. No computer. That was *very* bad news.

'How long till dinner, Mum?' Rory asked, sticking his head around the kitchen door.

'It'll be next week at this rate,' exclaimed his mother. Rory could see that she was looking stressed.

'What's wrong?' he asked.

'It's this stupid oven,' she said. 'That lightning strike must have done something to it. I can't get it to behave. Either it doesn't heat up at all, or it heats up too much! I've been trying to get it to work properly for over an hour now. And the hob is no better!'

Rory walked across the kitchen and twisted the control knob for the oven.

'Don't!' his mother said, snatching his hand away.

'I was just trying to – oh!' The rest of what he had intended to say was drowned by a loud fizzling sound – as if a big firework had been set off inside the oven. Then there was a hollow bang and black smoke began to filter out of the closed oven door.

Rory gave his mother an anxious look. 'Oops,' he said. 'Sorry.'

Mrs McBride opened the oven door. A moment later and the smoke alarm on the ceiling began to emit a piercing, beeping noise.

'Switch that thing off,' Rory's mum shouted. 'And I'll open some windows.'

Rory grabbed a broom and used the handle to press the 'reset' button.

Rory's father appeared in the doorway. 'Problem?' he asked.

'You'd better . . .' Mum began.

'. . . phone for a curry,' Mr McBride said, beating a hasty retreat.

Rory's mother sat at the kitchen table with her hand in her hands. 'This is all such a pain, Rory.'

Rory stood at her side. 'It'll be OK, Mum,' he said, patting her shoulder. 'Dad said the insurance should cover anything that's gone wonky.' He picked up the place mat from the table and wafted the smoke away. 'And it doesn't seem like anything else is messed up.'

As if in response to his words, a dull metallic rumble began to sound from the other side of the kitchen.

They both turned to look.

The washing-machine had started – with nothing in it. The red lights on the control panel were lighting up – blinking on and off at random as the empty barrel turned.

Rory quickly walked across the room and flipped the switch on the wall socket to the 'off' position.

The washing-machine continued to rumble away.

'How's it doing that?' he breathed, staring at the switch on the socket. He flipped it back and forth several times – but still the machine churned away under the work surface.

A few moments later, his mother's arm reached out past him and pulled the plug. The machine came to a sudden stop.

They looked at one another.

Rory was baffled. 'It carried on working after I turned the power off,' he said.

'There must have been some energy left in the cable,' his mother replied, her voice tight and strained.

He looked over his shoulder at the silent washing-machine. 'But that *can't* be right,' he murmured. 'Either the power's on, or it isn't.'

'Well – I fancy chicken korma,' she said with forced brightness. 'How about you, Rory?'

Rory stared at her.

She was trying to pretend it hadn't happened –

but it *had*. Electricity simply didn't behave like that – it was impossible. Rory had the creepy feeling that things were beginning to get out of control.

He wondered what was going to come next.

Rory was woken from deep sleep that night by a piercing electronic shriek. At first, he thought it was the smoke alarm again – but it was coming from close by.

He turned his head to look at his digital alarm clock. His eyes were still bleary from sleep, but he could clearly see the display flashing in the darkness of his room.

00:00

11:11

22:22

It was changing rapidly. In the stillness, the noise felt as if it were boring into his brain.

'Shut up!' he mumbled, slamming his hand down on the 'stop' button. The noise stopped – but it left a weird ringing in his ears. 'Stupid thing,' he grumbled, turning over and pulling the covers up over his ears.

Seconds later, the alarm's radio began to blare out. It was a foreign voice – a man talking excitedly. Annoyed, Rory threw the duvet back and switched on the bedside light. He pulled the radio alarm clock into his lap and rolled down the volume control until the voice was just a whisper.

As he lay back down, a thought struck him. He *always* kept the radio tuned to a music station. Changing it could have been a dumb joke of April's, but it didn't seem to be her style. Rory sat bolt upright and picked up the clock again. The digital display began to change more rapidly, speeding up until the red numbers were just a blur. It began to feel hot in Rory's hands.

Panicked, he dropped it on to the duvet, bunching himself up in a corner of the bed, watching the whirling numbers.

Gradually, the blur slowed.

The numbers came to a halt.

But they weren't numbers any more.

The display read the same thing as before: *RO:RY*.

Rory stared at the red letters, his heart pounding and a cold feeling growing in his stomach. *Not real. No way!* He closed his eyes and opened them again.

Now the fiery letters spelled out something else – something that brought Rory's heart up into his throat and made him gasp for breath.

The display read: *SO:ON*.

Trembling violently, Rory reached towards the clock. A crackle of blue sparks jumped from the machine to his fingertips – stinging him, making him cry out in pain. He clutched his hand to his body, frozen in absolute panic.

Staring down at the display, Rory hoped upon hope that the whole thing was a figment of his imagination.

03:15

A quarter past three in the morning.

Rory let out a gasp of breath. The nightmare was

over, but he was still shaking. He gave himself a few seconds to recover from the bizarre ordeal.

This is so weird, he thought. *What was that?*

He climbed out of bed and reached for the plug. He pulled it clear from the wall, and the display went out.

'I don't know if what just happened was real or not,' he murmured. 'But I'm not taking any chances.'

He picked up the dead alarm clock and wrapped the lead around it.

'You're going somewhere where you can't give me any more creepy messages, OK?' he said. He shivered slightly as he recalled first seeing the message on the front of the microwave the day before.

Were these things trying to tell him something?

But surely that's ridiculous? Rory's mind raced. He shook his head to clear it. Rory wasn't going to let thoughts like *that* into his head in the middle of the night. No way.

Bundling the alarm clock up in a pullover, Rory

stuffed it in the bottom drawer of his bedside chest and got back into bed.

The display *couldn't* really have spelled out his name. It *couldn't* have made words. That must have been his imagination working overtime.

But it was a long time before he managed to get back to sleep.

Rory padded into the kitchen, the tiles cold against his bare feet. It was early the next morning and he had not slept well after the incident with the alarm clock.

He stepped into icy-cold water.

He gave a startled yelp and stared down. A wide pool of water was spreading across the floor from the fridge.

'What are you yelling about?'

Rory looked around – April was standing in the kitchen doorway.

'There's cold water all over the floor,' Rory said. 'I think the fridge is bust.'

160

Their mother came up behind April. 'Oh, good grief,' she groaned, staring at the swimming floor. 'Is this never going to end?'

April was sent to fetch towels and the family mopped up the water and wrung it out into the sink while Mr McBride checked the fridge out.

He gave them a look. 'You're not going to believe this,' he said, opening the freezer compartment door, 'but it's actually hot inside here. The thing has gone haywire. We'll have to throw everything out.'

Mrs McBride sniffed the milk carton. 'Urgh – it's gone off,' she said. 'Rory – nip down to the shop and get us some milk, please.'

'And some orange juice,' April added.

'And you'd better get some butter, too,' said Mr McBride, handing Rory some money.

By the time Rory got back with the provisions, the table was laid for breakfast.

It was a dreary, miserable meal – just cereal and cold drinks and long faces all round.

'When are we going to get the electricity working properly?' April asked grumpily. She liked chocolate spread on toast for breakfast – but the toaster wasn't working.

Rory's dad got up and walked into the lounge. After a couple of minutes, he came back and sat down. 'I've called the electrician. He's all booked up today. The earliest he'll be able to come over is first thing tomorrow.'

'Can we watch TV?' April asked hopefully.

'I don't think we should use anything electric,' said her father. 'Just to be on the safe side.'

'*No TV?*' April gasped. 'That's it! I'm out of here.' She got up from the table and headed for the hallway. 'I'm going to spend the day at Rachel's.'

'I want you back here by five,' Mum insisted. 'You've got homework to do before school on Monday. Don't forget that your father and I are playing bridge round at the Sherwoods' this evening.'

'Yes . . . great . . . fine . . . *wonderful!*' April shouted as she stamped her way upstairs.

The Sherwoods. Rory groaned to himself at the very thought of them. They were the *most* boring of all his mum and dad's friends. When the four of them got together, they'd just sit playing cards for hours on end. *At least it's not Mum and Dad's turn to have them over*, he thought with some relief.

A minute or so later April came back into the kitchen. She was fiddling with her mp3 player and frowning. 'All my music's disappeared!' she said. She threw the gadget on the table. 'Is every single thing in this house useless now?' She glared at her father. 'Do you know how long it took me to download all my favourite tracks?'

'Can't you download them again from Rachel's PC?' Rory suggested. 'She's got the same mp3 player as you.'

'I *suppose* so, seeing that I don't have any other choice,' April said, crossly. 'Is it OK if I go over there now?'

Mrs McBride looked at her watch. 'It's only nine o'clock,' she said. 'Isn't it a bit early?'

'Rachel's mum won't mind,' April said, heading for the door. 'Besides, there's nothing to do around here anyway.'

'Homework?' her father tried.

'Housework?' Mum suggested, smiling.

'Nice try!' April said, laughing as she ran out of the kitchen.

The day wasn't as boring as Rory had feared. Despite the fact that all his mates had other things to do, he managed to keep himself quite happily occupied.

He passed a couple of hours helping his dad in the garden, tidying the hedges and pulling the weeds out of the flowerbeds. Then he disappeared up to his room to read a few of the comics that had stacked up over the past couple of weeks while he'd been too busy with his new driving simulation game. When his mother popped her head around his bedroom door to tell him she was going to phone for a pizza for dinner, he was surprised at how the time had flown by.

'Now, then,' Mrs McBride said as she cleared up after dinner. 'The cab is picking us up in a little while. The Sherwoods' phone number is on a Post-it note on the fridge door. If you need us, just call. And if it's really urgent, you're to go next door. Got that?'

'Yes, Mum,' Rory said. The next moment, he heard the front door open.

'I'm back!' April said, wandering into the kitchen.

'If you get peckish later, there are some snacks in the cupboard,' their mother told them. 'And once you've finished your homework, there are plenty of board games to keep you amused.'

'I'm going to wash my hair,' April announced. 'At least the hot water runs on gas. Can you imagine if we couldn't even have showers? Yuck!'

After his mum and dad had gone, and April was in the bathroom, Rory draped himself over the sofa and went back to his comics. There would be plenty of daylight to read by for another hour or so – and he was sure that his parents wouldn't be back that late.

About half an hour had gone by when his concentration was disturbed by a faint buzzing sound. He looked up, turning his head to identify the sound. It was familiar, but he couldn't place it.

After listening to the buzzing for a minute or so, he got up and opened the door into the hall. The noise grew louder. It was coming from upstairs.

Suddenly Rory realized exactly what it was that he was listening to.

It was a hairdryer.

'April!' he gasped, racing up the stairs. She had been told not to use *anything* electrical!

Rory pushed his sister's bedroom door open. 'April?' he called uneasily.

'Help me!' April croaked in a hoarse, fractured voice. She was bent double, struggling with the hairdryer. Rory felt terror grip him as he saw that a huge chunk of her wet hair was caught up in the dryer. The motor of the machine was growling and roaring, and the air was foul with the stench of burning hair. The lead of the dryer was somehow wound around his sister's neck.

Rory lunged forward, desperate to help. At that moment, she fell on to her side on the floor, clawing helplessly at the lead around her neck.

'It's strangling me . . .' she managed to force out, and Rory watched her face contort with fear and pain, her eyes bulging as the cord tightened around her throat.

'Hold on!' Rory shouted, and he dropped to his knees, snatching at the dryer. Fingers of smoke were rising up from April's scorching hair, and Rory's eyes began to stream from the thick, pungent smoke. He managed to get his fingers between April's neck and the hairdryer cord, but it seemed to twist and get tighter. All the while, it roared hysterically, as if it was filled with hostile life.

Rory could feel his heart pounding in his chest. His sister's face was going blue. He ran over to the wall and pulled the plug out of the socket.

The hairdryer went silent and crashed to the carpet like a dead thing.

April pulled the cord loose and curled up on the floor, her knees up to her chest, coughing and choking.

Rory found scissors on his sister's dressing-table and cut her hair to free her from the dryer. 'April?' He shook her. 'April! Are you all right? What happened?' He pulled her up into a sitting position. There was a nasty red weal around her neck. A few more moments and the cord would have choked her to death.

'I plugged it in,' April gasped. 'But the cable was all tangled up – and while I was trying to get the knots out, the thing turned on all by itself.' She stared wide-eyed at him. 'I tried to drop it – but it was like it was alive. It pulled itself right out of my hands!' She gulped. 'It went around my neck – and then my hair got sucked in.' She shuddered. 'It was so scary.'

'You're OK now,' Rory said. 'Can you get up?'

'Yes . . . I think . . . so,' she gasped.

'There's something really badly wrong with the house,' Rory said. 'We have to get out.'

April nodded. Rory helped her to her feet. 'Rory? What's happening?'

'I don't know,' Rory said, holding her steady. He stared into her frightened eyes. 'I don't think the lightning that hit us was *normal*. I think it's done something to the whole house.'

He helped April out on to the landing. From downstairs, he could hear loud music playing. It was the hi-fi system in the living-room – blaring out music at full volume.

Rory looked at his sister. 'The stereo isn't plugged in,' he said.

'It *must* be,' April gasped, staring down the stairwell. 'How could it do that if it's not plugged in?'

He looked at his sister and could see the growing terror in her face. 'We'll be OK,' he said, trying to sound as if he really believed it. 'I'll get us out of here, don't worry.'

More noise rang out from the TV room. Loud, distorted voices. The television burst into life, flicking through the channels – one after another, faster and faster.

'Come on,' Rory said, grabbing her hand. 'We'll go straight for the front door, OK?'

Hand in hand they ran pell-mell down the stairs.

April looked over her shoulder. 'What's that?' There was more noise – coming from the kitchen.

'Don't think about it,' Rory said. 'Run!'

Behind them, he could hear the rumble of the washing-machine, and other whirring and grinding noises – as if every electrical appliance in there had somehow burst into life, angry at them trying to leave.

Rory ran for the front door, pulling his sister along behind him.

He reached for the lock, but as he did, April shouted a warning.

'Rory! Look out!' she called.

There was a snapping sound as the bell cable that

ran up the wall alongside the door pulled itself out
of its staples and wrapped itself around the handle.
As Rory stared in disbelief, the broken end whipped
out towards him, lashing across his cheek.

Rory fell back with a yell of pain.

Blue sparks spat out from the lock. Rory gasped
as the end of the cable snapped in the air like a whip.

'Get away from it!' April shouted. 'We can use the
back door!'

Rory knew that meant going through the kitchen
with all its roaring and bellowing electrical devices
– but surely that had to be better than the snake-
like cables piercing the air to and fro.

'Yes! Go!' he gasped.

They ran for the kitchen – but the way to the
back door was blocked by what looked like a spider's
web of wires stretched across their path.

'What are we going to do!' screamed April over
the top of the tumult.

Rory had no idea. The radio and the portable TV
set were howling. The coffee grinder was whining

at full speed. The blender blades were whirring. The food processor was grinding away – and behind those sounds was the steady growl of the washing-machine and the shriek of the dishwasher.

Then Rory saw the digital display on the microwave. It was flashing rapidly.

RO:RY

SO:ON

RO:RY

SO:ON

'R . . . Rory?' April stared at the flickering display, and she began to scream.

Rory grabbed her and pulled her back out of the doorway as a fizzing wire came lashing towards them. He slammed the door, hearing the fierce *thwack* of the cable on the wooden door panels.

'April – stop screaming and think!' Rory shouted, dragging his sister's hands away from her face.

She stared at him, silent now, but panting with fear. 'We can still get out through the garage.'

The internal door to the garage was in a small

utility room that led off the hallway. Rory opened the door to the room. It was filled with shelving units stacked with his father's gardening equipment.

Rory took April's hand and pulled her into the room. They should be safe, he was pretty sure there wasn't anything electrical to attack them. He ran for the garage door and wrenched it open. There was a sudden surge in the noise from the rest of the house, bearing down on them from all sides, rising like an electronic chorus of rage.

The ceiling light burst on and off and the bulb exploded over their heads, spraying them with tiny shards of glass.

Rory and April ran through the door and slammed it shut behind them.

'What do we do now?' April gasped.

Rory ran alongside the car to the large metal garage door. It was the type that lifted up into the roof. He hammered the heel of his hand against the button that should open the door. There was a brief crunch of gears, but the door didn't move.

'Rory! Watch out!' April's voice was shrill with panic. A moment later, Rory threw himself backwards as a pair of thick cables wrenched themselves free of the wall and lunged towards him.

The fluorescent lights on the ceiling came on with a fizzing noise. Sparks showered down.

'Rory! What're we going to do now?' April shouted.

'In the car,' Rory replied. 'We'll be safe in there.' He snatched the car keys down off the rack by the door into the house. The car hadn't been anywhere near the house when the lightning had struck – it had to be a safe refuge.

His father had reversed the car into the garage to make for an easy start in the morning, so the front of the car was facing the big metal door. Rory opened the driver's door and the two of them bundled into the car. Rory slammed the door closed. April scrambled into the passenger seat, gasping for breath, her wide, frightened eyes staring out through the windscreen.

'We'll sit here and wait till Mum and Dad get home,' Rory said calmly. 'They'll know what to do.'

April looked at him. 'I'm not sure the car will protect us for that long,' she said. 'We might need to find our own way out.'

Rory gave a tight smile, desperate to reassure his sister. 'I'll think of something,' he said. He felt for the spare key under the seat.

As he found it and breathed a sigh of relief, there was a roaring and a clattering sound from the back corner of the garage. Rory twisted in his chair and peered through the rear window. He saw something rise up from under a plastic sheet. There was a grinding, rattling snarl as the thing lifted into the air.

'Oh, no,' Rory groaned. In an instant, he remembered what his dad kept back there.

'Rory,' April said, clutching his arm. 'What is it?'

'The hedge trimmers,' Rory said, cold sweat beading on his forehead.

The sheet finally slipped away and the grinding,

vibrating blades of the hedge trimmer were revealed. It stopped for a few moments, as if seeking out prey, then the long blade turned towards them.

The hedge trimmer smashed through the back window of the car, shattering it to a maze of pieces. The blade drew back and lunged again. Fragments of glass ricocheted around the inside of the car, but Rory saw that the cable was tangled up in something outside. The howling and clanking blade could not reach them.

'Rory!' April shouted. 'We have to get out of here, otherwise we'll be killed! You'll have to drive us out!'

Rory stared at his sister. He had never been behind the wheel of a *real* car. But he knew that April was right. At any moment, the tangled cable of the hedge trimmer could free itself – and then it would come crashing right through and puncture the front seats.

He pushed the key into the ignition and turned it.

The engine came alive immediately. *Thank*

goodness, Rory told himself. The new car was an automatic. He put it into 'drive', released the handbrake and pressed down on the accelerator.

His brain was in a whirl, but somehow he kept calm enough to get the car rolling forwards. The hedge trimmer slipped out of the back window and fell to the ground – but he could still hear the dreadful noise of it as it thrashed on the concrete. Swallowing a lump in his throat, he stamped down hard on the accelerator. The car leaped forwards with a jerk and banged into the large metal garage door with bone-shaking impact.

Rory winced as he saw the buckled and dented bonnet – the door was dented too, but it hadn't moved. The cables slapped against the car's windows.

'You have to hit it harder!' April shouted to him. 'Go faster!'

Rory managed to get the car into 'reverse'. It lurched backwards along the garage, catching the body of the hedge trimmer under the rear bumper and dragging it along the floor. The bladed machine's motor screamed in frustration. The car banged hard against the back wall before he could stop it. Summoning up all his courage, Rory put the car into 'drive' and slammed his foot down on the accelerator.

The car lunged forwards again, and Rory gritted his teeth as they hurtled towards the garage door.

There was a crash and crack of metal.

'You did it!' April said excitedly.

Rory watched as the door crumpled and the car made it through.

He looked at his sister. April's eyes were wide. 'You saved us!' she gasped.

'I did, didn't I?' Rory breathed, bringing the car to a halt on the front drive. He looked over his shoulder. The lights in the house were flashing rapidly on and off. It was as though the entire place was tearing itself to pieces in rage at their escape. Rory could see that neighbours were beginning to trickle out of surrounding houses, staring.

But they were safe now. 'Shall we walk from here?' he said, giving April a weak smile.

'I think that would be a *very* good idea,' April replied. She pushed at the door handle to get out. The door didn't move. 'It's stuck,' she said. 'We'll have to get out your side.'

Rory turned the keys and pulled them out of the ignition, but the low, steady purr of the engine didn't stop. 'That's weird,' he said to himself. He reached for the handle of his own door. As he did so, the central-locking button snapped downwards. 'What the—' Rory was cut off by something that filled him with renewed dread.

The sat-nav unit was back in its place on the dashboard.

And it was on.

April was staring at the brightly lit screen. 'Rory,' she said, her voice low and trembling. 'Did you do that?'

'It wasn't me,' Rory replied, his voice barely above a whisper. 'I didn't even know it was in here – Dad must have put it back.'

'Why has it come on?' April asked.

Rory swallowed hard. 'I don't know,' he said.

Before April could reply, a mechanical voice spoke. It wasn't the friendly female voice that they had heard before. It was a low, guttural, rasping voice that sent chills up Rory's spine.

'You wish to go to Dunbar Street,' it grated.

April looked at Rory. 'The voice . . . it's changed,' she said shakily.

The voice croaked again. *'From Howard Close you must turn left into Aynsley Avenue.'*

'Why is it telling us that?' April asked, her voice trembling.

'We have to get out of the car!' Rory shouted. 'Now!'

He fought desperately with the handle. The hideous voice spoke again, fiercer and more insistent now. *'You must turn left into Aynsley Avenue!'* it snarled.

Rory twisted in his seat and kicked at the door. In a moment, the car was backing up towards the garage.

'It's taking us back into the garage!' April screamed.

Suddenly, the car halted. The engine revved wildly, and Rory watched as the gear-stick flicked into 'drive' and the accelerator pedal slammed down to the floor. The car leaped forwards, pinning them in their seats. It crashed down the driveway and bounced down on to the road. The steering wheel spun. April and Rory were thrown to one side as the car careered along the road.

Rory grabbed the steering wheel in both hands, stamping down on the brake pedal. But the wheel spun in his grip, wrenching at his arms – and the brake pedal was useless.

The car began to gather speed, and April let out a scream as they narrowly avoided a head-on crash. The steering wheel spun at the last second and their car veered away from the impact. Rory heard the blare of car horns and the sound of shouting voices. He and April were travelling up the middle of the road, forcing other traffic to swerve and brake sharply to avoid them.

Rory stamped down again on the brake, but the car just kept accelerating. Rory clung to the wheel, terrified that at any moment they would crash headlong into some oncoming vehicle and be killed.

'Turn right into Ward Road,' the grating, mechanical voice roared.

The car lurched to the right.

'Where's it taking us?' April screamed.

Rory had no breath to reply – and no idea what the evil thing that was controlling the car was planning for them.

He tried once again to hold the steering wheel, but it was no good. It blistered his hands, and refused to move the way he tried to make it. Rory knew that he and April were completely helpless. He felt sick with terror. His mind clouded over with panic, and he slumped back into the seat.

Rory stared out through the windscreen. He knew where they were. The car had brought them halfway across town. Now all that remained was the blocked-off section of the road that led to the missing bridge.

His heart hammered against his chest. The sat-nav device was leading them straight to the broken bridge over the river.

April screamed as the car smashed through a wooden barrier.

As the car arced through the air, Rory could see the churning brown torrent of the river below. Just before they hit, they heard the rasping mechanical voice say one last thing.

'You have reached your destination.'